BRITISH
SHIPS

NEW JERSEY

Nancy Faulkner is both a meticulous historian and a superb storyteller, who knows how to maintain suspense to the last page. The author of *The Traitor Queen, The Sacred Jewel, Knights Besieged,* and many other popular books, Miss Faulkner brings the period and her characters vividly to life, whether she's writing about ancient Crete, 1st century England, 16th century Rhodes, or 18th century America. A graduate of Wellesley College, she received her M.A. in history at Cornell and later taught history at Sweet Briar College. Miss Faulkner now lives in New York City, where she pursues full-time writing career.

Jon Nielsen has been illustrating children's books for more than twenty-five years, and has a long list to his credit, including picture books, adventure stories, and the classics. Mr. Nielsen has a severe "wanderlust," he says, and he and his wife and small daughter spend part of each summer on camping trips, to Cape Cod, Appalachia, and Florida in recent years. During the rest of the year, they live in Dobbs Ferry, New York.

Deborah Stone brandished the stick menacingly at Johnny Darragh's tormentors, hoping to give the boy a few seconds to flee. Why was she risking her life for him, she wondered, when she'd seen him for the first time only today? How much she'd admired his outspoken pride in Washington's parading army just a few hours ago! But clearly, being a Patriot in 1777 in Tory Philadelphia was dangerous business, for Johnny's captors were threatening him with drowning.

15-year-old Deborah finds out for herself just how dangerous it is to be a Patriot. Alone in the war-swept city, with her beloved Uncle Matt in Washington's army and her mean and treacherous Aunt Sophy living out of town, she longed to do something for the Cause. But when, with Johnny Darragh, she had the chance to play a vital part in the Revolution, she realized how much courage was required —and wondered how really brave she was.

Nancy Faulkner has written an engrossing, suspenseful story of Tory-Patriot conflicts, of spies and secret messages, set against the vivid background of the American Revolution.

Other books by Nancy Faulkner

JOURNEY INTO DANGER

Nancy Faulkner

ILLUSTRATED BY JON NIELSEN

Garden City, New York

DOUBLEDAY & COMPANY, INC.

1966

Library of Congress Catalog Card Number 66–16326
Copyright © 1966 by Anne I. Faulkner
All Rights Reserved
Printed in the United States of America
First Edition

JOURNEY INTO DANGER

CHAPTER ONE

Deborah Stone wiped perspiration from her forehead and felt the burden of misery settle more closely about her. This had been a horrid day. The weather was hot and broody with thunderclouds hanging low in the west and threatening a storm that wouldn't break. Whatever she had tried to do since she got up this morning—and that time seemed about a hundred years away though it lacked an hour yet to noontide—had gone wrong. She felt heavy and awkward and huge as a giant. She was, she knew, over-tall for her fifteen years. Usually it didn't worry her. But sometimes she had what she called her big days when her feet and her hands, even her head, seemed to get in her way; seemed to tangle and bump and refuse to follow the orderly bidding of her mind. Today was such a day.

But, though her body was too big, her spirit felt shriveled and small. For days now whisperings and murmurings had come even to her secluded ears, whisperings that told of Tories hoping and praying that the British troops who had left New York were, indeed, coming to occupy the city of Philadelphia, which was her home. And, more distressing, were the whisperings of danger to the cause of freedom, a cause which had seized upon her heart to fill it to bursting with pride on that day, more than a year ago now, when she had stood in the Square and heard the ringing, triumphant, brave and exciting words of the Declaration of Inde-

1

pendence. She had found, upon that day for the first time, something outside her small daily concerns, something so much bigger than herself it was always present now somewhere in her mind, underlying all her other thoughts and coloring them. She had vowed upon that day to do *something*—she had not been able to say just what—to help the cause of freedom, and daylong and nightlong (for even her dreams were of helping) she had pondered what she could do. And she could think of nothing.

Today the consciousness of her failure seemed to shrink her very soul. What chance had she to strike even a small blow for that cause she had made especially hers, when the Woman wouldn't let her leave the house?

The Woman! Deborah's whole body shrank into itself at the very thought of the woman with whom she was doomed to spend her days. She was afraid of the Old Cow and that was the truth, sorely afraid.

Sometimes she could find a wry and secret pleasure in thinking of her hating names for Uncle Matt's cold and hard and ungiving wife. She wouldn't, she had decided on that day so long ago when Uncle Matt had brought her home with him, call the creature who looked at her with angry dislike Aunt Sophronisba. And she couldn't very well call her Mistress Albright. When she needed to name her to Uncle Matt she said "her." But to herself, her fat, sour-faced aunt-in-law was the Woman or the Old Cow, and she took some middling comfort from this private vengeance.

But not today. The Woman was on the warpath, as mean as a snake and as ugly-tempered as sin. Something, it seemed to Deborah, had got into her today. Something more than the usual petty tyrannies that made Deborah's days a kind of hell.

All morning the Woman had prowled about the house, to snarl at a bed not spread smooth enough or a trinket set back after dusting a quarter-inch out of its proper line. For the moment she was not in the small hot kitchen where Deborah was paring the first of the winter apples for a pie. But no telling when she would pounce again.

A board creaked somewhere and Deborah ducked her head and looked over her shoulder, fearful, shivering. But she was still alone in the room. If only Uncle Matt were here she would be safe. He loved her and made her feel wanted, not like an evil, crawling thing fit only to be stepped on and squashed. But Uncle Matt was the goodness knew where; somewhere on the roads that led away in all directions from Philadelphia into the countryside where people on farms had always some broken thing to be repaired by wandering tinkers such as Matthias Albright. He had been gone but two days on this trip. Likely he would not be home again until the end of the week. And only then would she feel safe from the persecutions of the Woman, from her abiding fear that one day those persecutions would cease to be small, nagging irritations and break out into something dangerous and deadly. For the Woman could be cruel. Deborah was certain of that; had seen the wish to hurt in the Woman's eyes and wondered why, so far, the wish had not fathered the act.

Deborah sniffed and wiped blurring tears from her eyes. But the tears wouldn't stay away and, seeing the

3

apple and the knife in her hands mistily through them, she felt the knife slip and cut, not the apple but her finger. The cut was not deep, though it was bleeding more than a little, and Deborah dropped the unpared apple into the bowl, went to the bucket for a dipper of fresh water to wash the cut and then to the open kitchen door to pour the water over her hand. She would, she was thinking, as she turned back into the kitchen, have to get a strip of linen from the pine chest in the hall to tie up the cut before she could get on with the apples. Pray heaven the Woman would not come until that was done.

She was crying in earnest now; crying because she was lonely and clumsy and had hurt herself and because she was so afraid and could not, in truth, find good reasons for her fear. She stumbled toward the door that led to the hall.

The Woman stood in the doorway, filling it with her fat, squushy body. She was glaring at Deborah, her squinched-up, ratlike eyes overbright with anger and hatred; her mouth that was too small for the rest of her face drawn into a hard, tight line. She took Deborah by the shoulder and spun her about, sending a shower of tiny blood drops from the still-bleeding finger spraying over the smooth stones of the kitchen floor.

"Where do you think you are going, Miss? Have I given you leave to stop your work and dawdle? It's little enough I ask you to do in my house. You might at least have the goodness to finish it."

Deborah couldn't speak, held in thrall to silence by the rat-shining of the Woman's eyes. She held out her hand, showing the cut and gestured to the blood drops

4

on the floor. The Woman looked at the cut and at the drops for a moment and the rage that had been waiting an excuse to break the thin bonds of control for more years than she could remember found it at last. Blood on her floor indeed.

The Woman took Deborah again by the shoulder and began to shake her, shrieking at her in the high, shrill voice of fury words Deborah didn't know the meaning of except to know they were of evil intent. Really terrified now and a little dizzy with the shaking, she tried to jerk away from the Woman and managed to loosen her hold. She started to go toward the outside door, toward escape from this madness, but her legs were shaking so much she could not get away. The Woman, with a silence now more threatening than her curses, had picked up a heavy wooden spoon from the table and was standing above the shaking Deborah who could not move beyond a cowering against the wall, crooking her arm above her head to protect it against the expected blows, too frightened to make a sound.

As if to underline her danger, thunder sounded far away and upon the heels of that sound came another, a human sound from the doorway that led outside. "What are you doing, Sophronisba Albright? Have I not told you to leave the child alone? Drop that spoon. At once, do you hear?"

The words whipped through the room and seemed to freeze the Woman in place. For three full seconds she stood holding the spoon, unmoving, not turning around, the raging eyes still fixed upon Deborah. Then, slowly, she dropped her arm and turned to face her husband.

"You have come too soon home, Matthias," she said in her normal, slightly whining voice.

Deborah, thinking Uncle Matt. It's Uncle Matt come home again. I'm safe, slid down along the wall until she was sitting on the floor having no strength left to stand. She put her face in her hands and shivered, weak with relief. She heard Uncle Matt talking, only half aware he didn't sound like the gentle, kindly uncle she knew.

"Go to the room, and wait there for me, Sophronisba, while I see to the child."

"She'll tell you lies, Matthias. She'll wind you about her finger as she always does, spoiled, feckless brat that she is, dropping blood on my clean kitchen floor, dawdling . . ."

"*Go!*" Uncle Matt did not raise his voice but the effect of the one word was as great as if he had thundered it, and Deborah heard through her haze the Woman's reluctant footsteps drag on the floor.

Deborah took her hand from her face and watched the tall, rail-thin man crossing the kitchen toward her. Seeing the concern upon his face, she managed the semblance of a smile for him.

"Did she hurt you, Deborah? Did she lay a hand upon you? If she did, by the Lord Harry, I'll—"

"I'm all right, Uncle Matt. She—she didn't hit me. Truly she didn't."

"What happened, child, to bring her to this—this wildness of anger?"

She told him of the cut finger though not of the fear and misery that had led to it. She wanted to put her head on his shoulder and blurt out all the tale of the

7

Woman's petty persecutions that had gone before and made living cheek by jowl with Sophronisba Albright a burden and a daily trial. But she had been so tempted before and had built in herself a strong wall against that temptation, remembering the day Uncle Matt had explained why he married the Woman. "Sophy," he said then, "Sophy can't seem ever to do more than put her worst foot foremost. She's a sad one, Deborah. I married her for pity. And I was wrong. Pity's hardly enough for a woman's whole life, and she broods. If she'd had children, now . . . but, there, no use harking after what wasn't to be."

She loved this quiet, slow-to-speak, gentle man who was the closest thing she could remember to a parent, and she would not hurt him—or have him think ill of her—not unless she was forced to. This was the first time in seven years the Woman had threatened her with bodily harm. Maybe this would not happen again and she must keep on bearing the daily miseries as she had borne them before.

Uncle Matt had helped her from the floor to his own armchair by the table and was examining the cut, clucking over it, soothing and calming her by his loving concern and his sympathizing words. "It's none so bad a cut, Deborah girl, but it had best be seen to, lest it fester and give you trouble later. Stay where you are while I find a healing herb salve and a bit of linen. And do you not fret about Sophy, child. I'll see she does not lift hand to you again. These rages come upon her now and then. The why of them I do not understand, but they do not happen often and I know a cure for them, so do you not fear."

He left her then and was back in a moment or two with the salve and linen and set about tending the small wound. While he worked he told her of his two-day journey and of how, finding a clock that needed repair and lacking some part for a proper job upon it, he had put the clockwork in his pack and brought it home to complete. Besides, he said, his last trips had been profitable beyond the ordinary and he was ready for any excuse to take a small holiday.

"I'm glad you came," Deborah said. And he laughed, though the sound was grim and not mirthful, and said, "I'd not be doubting that, child, and none too soon either. There! The cut will mend now."

"I'd best get back to the apples," Deborah said, wanting to give the Woman no further and just cause for complaint against her.

He started to protest and sighed and stopped himself. "Yes," he agreed, "maybe it would be best if the cut doesn't hurt too much."

"It doesn't hurt at all," she said, thinking likely the hurting would come later when the real healing began. She got up and found the shaking had stopped and she could move naturally enough to the bowl she had left. Uncle Matt watched her a moment before he said, "I'd best get on to Sophy," and left. Deborah deliberately concentrated her thoughts upon Uncle Matt to keep at bay the nagging doubts that he could, in truth, hardly control the Woman when he was away. He'd said he was due a holiday, so for now, for a while, she would be safe. No use to borrow trouble. Yet, no matter how hard she tried, uncertainty and depression stood beside her as she worked.

CHAPTER TWO

"Can you see them, Uncle Matt? Are they coming? Oh, why don't they *hurry?*"

Deborah's brown curls were blowing around her face as she stood on tiptoe and leaned out from the first rank of watching, waiting people who made a thin line along the street.

"Possess your soul in patience, Deborah girl. Takes a time and a time for ten thousand marching souls to reach a place. They'll come, do you not fear."

Uncle Matt stood inches higher than anyone near him. His plain, laughing face reflected her excitement but he stood quietly enough. Deborah caught his arm and squeezed it hard. She *was* glad all over again and for a happier reason that he had come home.

Excitement so filled her she forgot, for the first time in days, her sense of frustration that she was entirely inadequate to take part in the fight for freedom. Here and now she seemed, in some mysterious way, to *be* taking part. But if Uncle Matt hadn't come, she knew she would not be standing here on this Sunday in August in the year 1777 in the city of Philadelphia. She savored the words in her mind, liking the rolling sound of them. The Woman, having little liking for parades and less for the Continental Army and General George Washington, would never have let her come out to watch. She shivered with the fear of the Old Cow, which never quite left her. She shook herself a little and the shadow of a smile chased the hating look from her gray eyes.

Well, it didn't matter. Not today when the British army was still, evidently, far away. Not this glorious morning, already muggy hot, when she was here with her beloved Uncle Matthias waiting for General Washington to show his army to the British-loving, business-as-usual-and-a-pox-on-the-War-for-Independence people of Philadelphia. She wondered how long Uncle Matt would stay at home this time, turned to ask him and held her question for she heard distantly and thinly borne on the small morning wind, the rattle of drums and the high fluting of fifes.

"They're coming! They're coming! They're coming!" she cried, and heard her words punctuated by a ragged cheer from somewhere farther up the street.

The quickstep music came nearer. Uncle Matt shifted his feet and pounded the big cobblestones before them with the heavy thorn stick, part weapon, part cane, he carried on his travels. She could feel excitement running through him as she clutched his arm and leaned forward again.

"Look!" she said softly, as two men on big, side-stepping horses came into clear focus out of the distance, riding boot-to-boot.

The man on the white horse looked huge. Sunlight slanted across immaculate blue coat and buff knee breeches and picked out the sheen of polished leather boots. His face was tired and stern though there was more than a hint of kindness in it. Now and again, unconsciously, he twisted his mouth a little as if it hurt him.

11

The rider beside him sat his sorrel mare with grace
and elegance. He was less tall in his saddle than the
other but no less proud. His eyes moved quickly over
the people as he turned his head from side to side.

Uncle Matt said loud and clear and pridefully, "May
God bless you, General George Washington, and you
too, Marquis de Lafayette."

A hundred and fifty yards behind their leaders a
troop of light-horse led by a subaltern, his sword
winking in the sun, rode smartly. Each man was
dressed according to his fancy, and, though many of
the coats and breeches showed threadbare in the clear
morning light, all were well brushed and worn with
an air. Each man in the troop, as did all those who
came after, wore in his three-cornered hat or cloth

cap, a sprig of green as evidence they were all one
army.

The light-horse troop was followed by two hundred
guards and another troop of horse. There was then a
space of two hundred yards empty of marchers, before
two more mounted regiments passed and, after another
one hundred yards of emptiness, a foot company of
pioneers in brown hunting shirts, carrying axes with
blades so bright they hurt the eyes.

As the pioneers passed, someone behind Deborah
spoke softly but clearly, "Look at them! Ragtag and
bobtail strung out like fish on a string after a poor
catch to make a show. Scarce a decent uniform among
them. And every man for himself in the matter of
weapons. Zounds, does his high-and-mightyness Geor-

gie-Porgie Washington think to fight Sir William Howe's army when it comes with that starveling rabble?"

Deborah's face grew red with anger as men and women behind her muttered agreement with the speaker. Stupid Tories, she thought—and added in her mind as she heard a man's voice saying, "Indeed thee is right, Jonas,"—and Quakers. How could any man or woman living in the colony—no, the *state*—of Pennsylvania take the part of the British? How could they sit back in their rich homes wearing their rich clothes and eating their rich food and fail to see they were little more than slaves to wicked King George? She turned to send a look she hoped would show her loathing at the people behind her. A man in a dark green coat with a fall of finest linen at his throat said, "Mark the little filly. Must be a rebel for she'd kill us with her looks if she could." He laughed and the laughter further infuriated Deborah and she opened her mouth to tell the stranger what was in her mind, forgetting her age and the manners she'd been so carefully taught.

Uncle Matt stopped her. He put his hand lightly on her arm and stooped to whisper in her ear, "Do you be quiet, Deborah girl, and be careful. It's not—*safe* to call attention to your patriotism in this city of king-lovers."

Before Deborah could ask him to explain what he meant he spoke aloud—to the loyalists behind him though he kept his head turned toward the parading Continental Army. "Do you mind, Deborah, how I told you once of the British General Braddock in the years gone by, leading his spic-and-span army right

14

smack into an ambuscade of yelling, murdering Indians; and of young George Washington, little more than a lad indeed, and his handful of *ragtags* and *bobtails* who did whatever fighting was done that day for the British? Reckon it's not the uniform makes the soldier, as many a redcoat at Princeton and Trenton learned this Christmas past. Those lads yonder—their arms are right well burnished and they carry them like the soldiers they are. Reckon they might in truth face an equal number of General Howe's with a reasonable prospect of success."

"Bah!" said the man who had laughed at Deborah; but there was, for all that, no more open sneering at George Washington's army. Uncle Matt's shots, she judged, had gone well home. She wondered briefly why it was safe for him to speak so when she must be quiet, but this was no time for wondering when General Washington's men were parading before her very eyes.

She was so absorbed in watching the passing men, in listening to the drums and fifes placed in the center of each brigade, in seeing how easily the soldiers kept the time of the moderate quickstep, she hadn't noticed her uncle's increasing restlessness. He had to say her name twice in her ear before he could draw her attention back to himself. When he had it, he thrust his thorn stick at her and said, "Got an errand I just thought of. Stick'll do nothing but hinder me in the crowd. Bring it home when parade's done."

Taken by surprise, Deborah hadn't quite caught the stick and had dropped it to the cobbled street. She had bent to pick it up while he was still talking and,

15

as she straightened, she said, "Uncle *Matt!* What errand? You *can't* . . ." But she was talking to air, for he had already pushed through the people behind him and disappeared.

Deborah was puzzled and more than a little disappointed. Uncle Matt had taken such pride in this army, had cheered louder than anyone when Colonel John Nixon had stood on the platform raised in the State House yard a time ago by the men who watched the stars and read out the Declaration of Independence, had talked long and often about the rights and freedom of men due the people of America and denied them by the British. Why would Uncle Matt leave before the parade was over?

A swirl of music from another set of fifes and drums interrupted her brooding and drew her mind back to the marchers. They were playing "Yankee Doodle" now as if they had heard the Tory remarks and were ridiculing them, making a triumphal march out of the singing japes the British soldiers had thrown at the Colonial troops so short a time ago. General Muhlenberg's brigade was passing. She wanted to shout "Hurrah," but without Uncle Matt beside her to bolster her resolve she felt curiously shy and lacked the courage to raise the cheer against the sullen and smothering silence of the people about her. The devil, the devil, the *devil!* she thought. I wish I were a man and could do something for our cause instead of a silly, useless girl. She wished somebody would shout— or something.

As if her thought had worked what she wanted, a single voice near her said, "Hurrah! Hurrah! *Hooray!*"

16

She looked toward the sound and saw a boy she judged to be about her own age step out from the curb waving and grinning like an agitated monkey. He was watching the first rank of Muhlenberg's men as if his eyes were attached to it by a string. She didn't realize she was, herself, grinning until the boy seemed to sense some sympathy in her. He took his eyes away from the men for a moment and looked at her and said, with enormous pride, "That's my brother! See the lieutenant beside the first rank."

She looked where he had pointed and saw an alert, thickset yet graceful young man, marching poker-straight beside his men. Only the smile he couldn't quite keep from his lips acknowledged the encouragement of his young brother.

Deborah turned to speak to the boy but he was gone. She looked ahead and saw him running along the street to catch up with the file of men flanked by his brother. When he was just opposite he fell into the quickstep rhythm of the music as if he'd been born to soldiering. Only then did she realize, with surprise, that he was dressed in the sober clothes worn by the members of the Society of Friends. What on earth was a Quaker doing in the Continental Army? She'd always heard fighting was dead against their religion. Indeed, Uncle Matt had told her, some were so peaceable they refused even to promise to abide by the orders of the Continental Congress.

The rumble of artillery turned her attention once again to the parade and drove all thought of the strange boy from her mind. She stood watching, then, until the last of the light-horse that formed the rear guard of

17

Washington's army had gone on its way out of sight toward the Chester Road on the way back to their camp. She hoped that this display of the General's forces had impressed the Tories as Uncle Matt had said it was intended to do. Then, a little sadly, for the passing of a parade brings always a feeling of regret, she took firm hold on Uncle Matt's heavy stick and started to the house near the wharf lent to Uncle Matt by his prosperous farmer brother, Cyrus.

The small, snug house had been home to Deborah Stone for the seven years since her father and mother, Uncle Matt's sister, had died of the pox within a few hours of one another. She thought of them little; indeed she could just barely remember them and would have forgotten them altogether had not Uncle Matt kept them in her mind by talk of them.

The streets were mostly empty. The people who had lined them had hurried to their homes to ready themselves for church or meeting. The small wind had grown stronger and stirred the leaves, already beginning to fall, and the flotsam always left behind by a crowd. There would likely be thunder before nightfall.

She had passed the mouth of a dark little alley that ran between two shops, closed and shuttered for the Lord's day, before she heard jeering voices and laughter that had a cruel sound. What was going on in there? Common sense told her to go on her way for it was no concern of hers. But curiosity, always stronger than sense in her, bade her investigate, and she turned back.

In spite of the deep shadows in the alley, she could see well enough, a ring of backs belonging to boys of various heights and thicknesses, slovenly boys with the look of street urchins without proper bringing up. They were shouting something in unison and, at first, she couldn't make out the words. Then, as her mind absorbed the rhythm of the chant, she began to distinguish the matter of it.

> Johnny Darragh
> Is a coward
> Fraid to fight
> With main and might.
> Fraid cat!
> Fraid cat!
> *Fraid* cat!

Who or what was Johnny Darragh?

CHAPTER THREE

Deborah took a step further into the alley and craned her neck trying to see beyond the ring. Then one of the boys shifted his position and made a window in the human wall. Through the space she saw the boy who had cheered for his brother standing with his back almost touching the brick of the shop. His clothes were mussed and dusty, his mouth was set in a tight line and his hands were balled into fists, but he made no move against his tormentors.

One of the boys, the tallest and heaviest, held up a hand and the chanting stopped. "Come on, Johnny Darragh, fight. You can choose the smallest of us. Come on. Just one little scrap and you can go home to your mo-other."

"Thee knows I'll not fight."

Deborah watched, unseen, the baiting of the boy whose name was Johnny Darragh. She wondered why he didn't take up the challenge and be done with it. He was as tall as his tormentor and looked to be even stronger. Likely Johnny would come off best in a scrap. At the worst he would have a black eye and a bruise or two which would mend quickly enough. *Why* wouldn't he fight?

Likely, she told herself, he deserves what he's getting. Likely he *is* a coward. And she was sorry because she had liked the boy and she had little use for cowards. She judged the others would leave him alone when they tired of their teasing. She'd best be on her way. She was turning to go when the tall boy spoke again.

"Why? Why won't thee fight, Johnny Darragh? Thy fine big brother's ready enough to take arms against his rightful king! The Darraghs have forgot, likely, the teaching of the Friends."

The quality of the tall boy's voice had changed as he spoke of Johnny Darragh's brother. Light and teasing at first it had become hard and tight and full of venom. The other boys drew their circle a little away as if some new thing had come among them. Johnny Darragh seemed to have taken courage from the mention of his brother. He moved a little away from the wall and stood very straight. Deborah stayed where she was.

"Thee well knows I won't fight thee," Johnny Darragh went on so softly the words hardly reached Deborah's ears. "Being a Friend thyself, thee knows it is not permitted."

"Then what about thy fine brother, Johnny Darragh? Seems *he's* willing enough to fight."

"And why shouldn't he take arms in defense of justice and freedom for free men?" Johnny's voice strengthened and he looked straight at the boy who seemed to be the leader of the group. "It's none the same thing."

The ring had broken now and Deborah could see the faces of the boys who had made it. Just ordinary boys, taking pleasure in badgering one who was not quite like them. All but one, the one who had spoken. His face was livid, his mouth working though no words came from it. A little spittle formed in one corner and began to drool down his chin. Deborah thought he was one easily possessed by anger, and therefore dangerous.

One of the others, tired of waiting for an answer to the question, said, "Because you're *Quakers*, that's why. Because everyone knows it's against the Quaker religion to fight."

Deborah was puzzled. She knew little about the religion of the Friends beyond knowing that many of the people of Philadelphia held to it and wore, as Johnny Darragh wore, the plain gray clothes that distinguished those who belonged to the Friends' Meetings. She was not, in truth, much concerned with religion beyond the simple truths of mercy and justice, honesty and love Uncle Matt had taught her. She did not much hold with fighting, for it had never seemed to her to settle anything. But surely there could be no great harm in protecting yourself when you were in danger. Still, it was plain Johnny Darragh was no coward. Indeed, she thought, it would take more courage to refuse to fight because of what Johnny believed than to do so. To her liking for him, formed instinctively when he had so eagerly and lovingly cheered his brother in the march, was added a deep respect. She sighed a little as she turned her attention back to the scene she was watching.

Johnny Darragh lifted his chin. "It is surely wrong to fight in anger or for thine own protection or profit. But it is not wrong to defend a great cause—a great *idea*, to fight against tyranny or evil if thy—thy inner light tells thee to."

The boys were silent. This kind of thinking was beyond them. Johnny's words had interrupted the spirit of their gamesomeness and they shifted about uncertainly, disappointed, wondering what to do next. One or two of them were obviously ready to give the whole thing up and go home.

Then the one who was their leader spoke. His voice came hoarse and rasping as if he were only with difficulty able to push it through the rage that still filled his throat. "And does thy inner light say it's right and just for your Continental Congress to send peaceful men to far-off foreign places because they won't support this—this fight? I see thee knows"—the words were coming more easily—"what I mean. Thee knows of those good men, leaders of the Friends' Meetings, even now being treated as—as vermin while they wait to be sent to some Godforsaken place a many a mile from home because they won't promise to support that cause thee prates of. My own uncle, though he is ill and feeble and may never live to come home again, is with them, Johnny Darragh. Thee calls *that* justice and freedom?"

Johnny shifted his weight from one foot to another. "Thee does not understand," he said. "The fight for freedom—it's bigger than any one man. The Friends who are being sent away—and only to Virginia, not some foreign land—would likely help the British if they could, and they have only to promise not to hinder the Cause, not to help the enemy. They're not asked to fight. Nobody—"

The big boy didn't hear him out. "Come on," he shouted, seeing the others becoming bored by the talk, seeing them losing interest in what was to them no more than a way to pass an idle hour on a Sunday morning, "come on. Let's teach this rat some manners. Let's run him to the wharf and duck him in the river. That'll likely cool his fondness for patriots!"

The others found their interest again quickly. This was more like it. This was what they were here for. This was good. "Come on, then," they shouted, their voices full of glee, "to the river."

The blood had gone out of Johnny's face. "Please," he said, and the thin sound of despair cut beneath the jubilant shouts, "please. I'll drown. I cannot swim."

His tormentors jeered at him. "Can't swim! That's silly. Course you can swim. Anybody can swim if he has to."

They began to move toward him, keeping in a tight group, reaching for him with their hands already crooked to grasp his clothes.

Deborah felt herself shaking all over. They were going to *drown* that boy. Once more he shrank against the wall as if he would will it to open and let him through, and, as the yelling boys pressed in upon him to haul him bodily to the river, she knew she should do something to help him. But she could not force herself to move and she realized with shame that she was afraid. What right had she ever had to judge others' fears as she had, just now, judged Johnny Darragh's? *She* was the coward.

She looked wildly along the alley, praying for someone to come and stop this baiting. But the whole way was quiet and empty.

She was shaking more and more and the shaking reminded her of something; of the way she had shivered when the Woman stood over her yesterday with the wooden spoon raised to beat her. Shivered with fear. She felt that fear again as if she were back in the kitchen, and looked at Johnny and saw the same feeling reflected in his eyes. She thought he must be feeling as I felt then, and she knew a sense of identity with him in his terror that outweighed her own cowardice. A surge of strength she'd never known before rose in her and brought with it joy and resolution and a new power to assess this situation with coolness and calm.

None of the boys was yet aware of her presence. She just might be able to surprise them and so give Johnny Darragh the time he needed to get away. She shifted Uncle Matt's stick until she held it as a bar, parallel to her body and chest-high; took a deep breath and shouted with all the force she could pull from her lungs, "*Stop!*"

The effect was immediate. The boys' heads turned as if they were one head and for a second or two they

stared at her with their mouths hanging stupidly open. Johnny Darragh could have escaped them easily but he didn't move. What ailed the fool? Couldn't he see this was his chance? She didn't know how long she could hold them, for even now the opportunity made by surprise was gone. The leader was shouting, "What ails thee, dolts? Stop staring. It's only a girl! To the river!"

The boys started once more toward Johnny, turning their backs to Deborah as if she didn't exist. Because I'm just a girl, she thought, furious that they should so ignore her. She'd show them.

She dashed toward the nearest boy and, swinging the stick, gave him a buffet on the shoulder that spun him around, causing him to stagger a little. He let out a howl and reached for her but she had already stepped back and was again holding the stick before her as a shield. Once more the other boys had stopped to see what was happening. They looked now to their leader, wondering what he would do in the face of this continuing and, indeed, increasing threat from the girl. That showed them, she thought with satisfaction.

The tall boy began to come toward Deborah, carefully, step by step, his face screwed into a menacing expression he intended to be horrible but which Deborah found so funny she had to fight down a fit of giggling. She held the stick toward him and said, steadily, "Be careful. It's a good cudgel and I well know its use."

He stood in his tracks and looked around the knot of his followers. He was, she thought, sending them some order, willing them with his eyes to come to his

26

aid: to rush her, likely, since he was too canny to face
the stick alone. She backed slowly toward the alley's
narrow mouth so they could not come at her from all
sides at once. She called to Johnny Darragh as she
moved, "Run!"

He said, "No! I am *not* a coward. I won't run."

"Don't be a fool!" she called furiously, wondering
what on earth was the matter with him. "Do you want
to drown then? It's six to one against you. Run!"

Out of the corner of her eye she saw the knot of
boys beginning to inch toward her. She said, "The first
one of you to come near enough will feel the cudgel,
I promise you."

The movement stopped and she shouted again to
Johnny, "Run! Run, stupid. *Fast!*" She gulped with relief as he pushed himself away from the wall with his
hands. She moved a little then to give him passage
from the alley and stood facing the others, making
pushing movements at them with the stick. She felt a
light touch on her back and, a moment later, heard the
welcome sound of boots thudding on cobbles, and
backed out of the entrance, shifting the stick as she
went and swinging it with both hands as a club.

She wondered if the boys would rush her now and
felt the taste of fear and thought of a ruse that might
hold them a moment or two longer. The narrow back
street was empty but she yelled toward the alley,
"Constable! Come quickly!" and hoped her pretense
would work long enough to let her get away.

She didn't stay to know what the boys would do but,
in her turn, ran swiftly until she came to the main

street that bordered the river and saw with relief people strolling along it.

She crossed the roadway and stood pretending to watch the river while she stilled her breathing and waited for her heart to stop its wild pumping. When she was a little rested she went on. Her body was shaking with anger and relief but her mind was curiously light. She was almost happy for the first time she could remember—the first time when she had not been surrounded by the love and protection of Uncle Matt's presence beside her.

Why? What's happened to me? Then suddenly, as if the sun had come out from under some rain cloud and shone right into her mind, she knew. She had, for once, conquered fear; had stood right up to six boys bent upon mischief and come through unhurt; had even spoiled their wicked plans.

She wouldn't pretend to herself that it would last, that she would, because of this day, be forevermore unafraid of the Woman. But she would have less fear of her own lack of courage because once she had seen her cowardice clear and true and taken action in spite of it. Maybe the next time the Old Cow threatened her she would be a little stronger.

She wondered, as she walked on toward the small gray house, what had become of Johnny Darragh. Once started he must have rivaled the wind in his going, for she'd seen neither hair nor hide of him in the back street. Nor were his red head and sturdy, gray-clad body among the people here. He must have gone the other way out from the alley. She would like to see him again, to know more about him, for he interested her. No matter. Philadelphia was none so large a place and now Uncle Matt was home he would, if she asked, take her about the streets and she would surely run across Johnny Darragh again. Uncle Matt might even know him—or his parents.

She had come to the small house and the door was closed. Strange, she thought with a sense of disquiet. On summer days it usually stood wide to let whatever air might be stirring blow through the narrow hallway to cool the kitchen at the back. She eased the door open, cautiously, wanting to avoid the Old Cow if she could. She heard a sound, shrill, angry, from the kitchen and tiptoed along the hall until she could pick out words.

". . . thinking of," the Woman was shrieking, "to go off and leave me alone with your brat of a niece and no one to get food for my mouth or firewood to warm me?"

"Now, Sophy." Uncle Matt's voice was calm, soothing, but it was lost at once in the torrent of her anger.

"Continental Army is it? For the whole war too and the dear knows how long that will be. You couldn't even go for a short term in the militia like any sensible man if so be any soldier is ever sensible? What have you to do with the Continental Army? You be needed here, not off somewhere pretending to a soldiering you're far too old for. You'll not do it, I say. You'll *not.*"

"Ah, but I will, Sophy. I have." There was nothing soothing in the sound of Uncle Matt now. "No, you *will* hear me."

Deborah edged closer and peeked around the doorframe to see what was happening. Uncle Matt's hand was covering the Woman's mouth as he held her pudgy body easily against the white plastered kitchen wall. "A man must do what a man must do, and this war and its aims are my business, my duty, for I believe in liberty and freedom. And what a man believes he must be willing to fight for. It's true you don't hold with independence but love the old ways and would kiss the very feet of Evil George did you but have the chance. Yes, even though he's set *Indians* to kill your own countrymen and women. Well, it's your right to follow your own mind's leading, though it be a stupid mind and tight closed to sense. But you'll not hold me from *my* right. Not if you yammer from now till Christmas comes. Old I may be—though there be a plenty older in this fight—but I've better legs and stronger than many a youngun' in the ranks and what's a gun on the shoulder to a man well used to carrying packs twenty times heavier than a long rifle? As to your living, there'll be enough and to spare when I've traded what's in my pack, to keep you and the girl till snow flies. Then you can go to my brother Cyrus who'll see you both safe enough and fed and warm till I come home again. What's done is done, Sophy. I've 'listed for the war and so soon as I make all secure here I'll be going to General George Washington himself for my orders. *Ouch!*"

Deborah saw him jerk his hand away and put it in his mouth and guessed the Woman had bitten him.

"No you don't, Matthias Albright!" the Woman said. "Oh, no you don't. For I'll *not* go to your brother Cyrus to be no more'n a slave to his prating wife. I'll

30

not *go,* do you hear? And you'll not leave *your* lawful wife, I'm thinking, *nor* that apple of your eye Deborah, to starve and freeze the long winter through. You can just march yourself right back and un'list."

Uncle Matt stood very still, looking at her for a long time while Deborah held her breath wondering what his answer would be. She was torn between pride in Uncle Matt as a soldier in the Continental Army and dismay at the thought of living with the Woman without the protection of his sudden and unexpected returns from his trips. At last Uncle Matt said in a voice so quiet and yet so deadly it sent a chill along her back, "Do as you will, Sophronisba. For these ten years I've tried to cherish you as a husband should, though there've been times it near killed me. Now I am going. Going to stand up for the things *I* believe in. If you don't want to spend a comfortable winter with Cyrus and his family—safe and warm and fed in return for helping his wife with her chores—you can stay here and make do as best you can. Maybe your friends the British, when they come—and they surely are coming— will look out for you. If you won't go, you won't. Then I shall take Deborah to Cyrus tomorrow and you will see me no more—ever. It's for you to decide."

Deborah, watching the woman, feeling—almost—a little sorry for her, saw the high color leave her face; saw her hands go out toward Uncle Matt, fluttering; saw a look of panic come into her eyes. "You—you *wouldn't,* Matthias. You wouldn't leave me forever?"

Uncle Matt's face twisted with the inner struggle between his gentle nature that would always avoid hurting and some new-found, strong and stubborn core

31

in his heart. His hands twisted at his side and Deborah thought she saw tears in his eyes but he said, steadily, "Yes, Sophy, I would. I—I *must* if you seek to hold me from that thing I have to do."

The Woman made a dead, hopeless sound that wasn't quite a sob. "Very well. It shall be as you say. I will go to your brother before the snow flies." She ran from the kitchen and Uncle Matt let out his breath in a great sigh and sat heavily in the chair nearest to him.

Deborah ran into the room and knelt beside him. He didn't see her. He was staring straight ahead, his face troubled and sad, his hands shaking a little. She touched his arm and said, "Uncle Matt. You're going to be a soldier. I'm glad. Oh, I'm *glad*."

CHAPTER FOUR

Uncle Matt was gone two days later, gone to General Washington's headquarters on the Skippack Road. He had promised her before he left that the Woman would not dare mistreat her again for fear of his wrath when he should return. And he had warned her, once more, to have a care how she showed her fervor for General Washington and the freedom army. Philadelphia was becoming, Uncle Matt explained, each day more a city of king-lovers. Many of them were decent-enough men, willing to let alone the few patriots among them, so long as those patriots did nothing to hurt the British cause. But there were some among them not only willing but eager to harm those they called rebels. If the

British came to take over the city those squinched-up, mean-minded men would think nothing of reporting rebels or even suspected rebels to them. Deborah had promised to be careful, thinking dolefully enough, he'd no need to worry. She'd have small chance to show her sympathies with the Woman to act as jailer.

She kept out of the Woman's way, did her chores quietly and as well as she could, though there was no pleasing the Woman's finicking demands. But misery stalked her and came one day to rest so heavily upon her spirits she went to the far corner of the kitchen where the spinning wheel stood always ready, thinking its familiar, rhythmic whir might comfort her.

The kitchen, usually a bright and cheerful place, was today as heavy as her heart, for clouds hung gray and low in the sky and seemed to press like a great, sad face against the small, leaded panes of the window. For a while the linen thread twisted smoothly onto the spool as her foot pressed the treadle evenly and her right leg steadied the twirling spindle. But the merry whirring of the wheel failed to ease the troubled thoughts that tumbled through her mind. Pity for herself depressed her and divided her attention.

Uncle Matt had gone out of her life as surely as if he were dead from a British bullet. She well knew he might, indeed, be killed. But even if he survived the fighting he would likely not come home again until the war was done and, as the Woman had said, the dear knew when that would be. If she could only have gone with him. If she could only have been a boy instead of a niggling, useless girl she could by now

33

be taking a part, a real part, in this revolution against tyranny.

She didn't know she had relaxed her pressure on the spindle until the sound of the slowing wheel warned her of trouble and she realized too late to avoid catastrophe that the fine thread was a tangled mess. She stopped the wheel and set to work to try to repair the damage. Tears she couldn't keep from running blurred her sight and her hands trembled in their hurry to make all right before she should be caught.

Slap. Slap. Slap.

Her first sense that the Woman was in the kitchen came when her ears rang with the full weight of a savage boxing. Pain followed quickly, so stinging she heard the words hurled at her as if they came from a great distance.

"Ungrateful, clumsy, hateful wretch," the Woman was shouting. "Isn't it enough that I must bear your presence in my house without having the work ruined? I'll not have it, do you hear? I'll not have it. Your weak-kneed, pusillanimous uncle isn't here for you to look to now, my girl. No chance he'll be sneaking in at any moment so you can run to him with your tales against me. No. You've me and only me to reckon with now and I'll not put up with your lackadaisical ways. And do you not forget that. It's spoiled you are, spoiled rotten by your uncle who sees in you nothing but the living image of his beloved sister gone these seven years. You'll get no quarter from me, miss. You'll learn what it's like to feel discipline. Now get out of my sight while I put right your fecklessness. *Get*."

Deborah stumbled up, her ears still hurting from the heavy blows. She was half blind with tears of anger and pain and uneasiness. She went to the woodshed and crouched on the earthen floor, holding her ears with her hands and crying as she had never cried before. Gradually the pain went away and the crying trailed off to an occasional sob or sniffle and she settled more comfortably into her place. Fear still threatened her, threatened to throw her again into mindlessness, until she thought of the boy she had rescued and took heart, remembering how she had found courage to do what she had feared to do.

What could she do? The Woman had made it plain enough she would vent all her hidden venoms, especially her venom against Uncle Matt's enlistment, upon his niece. Deborah shivered, thinking what hard things could come to her in the long weeks before the cold weather really set in. It was only the beginning of September. Even if the weather, bringing winter early, worked for her she couldn't hope to go to the farm for weeks. If only the wood would give out or the food. But the neat stacks behind her were more than enough to provide fire until the hard cold came. The larder was well stocked and Uncle Matt had even left a purse heavy with shillings he'd somehow persuaded Evan Hunter to give him for some of the goods in his pack.

There was only one thing to do. She'd have to get away from here. She doubted the Woman would care much. Good riddance, she'd likely think. But where could a girl of fifteen go, how find her own keep in this town already nervous with rumors that the British were coming? Uncle Matt had said that before long there'd be scarce a patriot left in Philadelphia. She could go now, by herself, to the farm across the river. But Uncle Cyrus was not like Uncle Matt. Older, harder, less kind, he too had called Uncle Matt simple-minded for burdening himself and his wife with a girl child when there were places, right here in Philadelphia, where she could be cared for at no expense to Matthias Albright. Uncle Cyrus, if she went to him, would surely not believe her story, would surely send her back straightway. The farm was no good for her escape.

Where then? What *could* she do?

She had got so far in her thinking when she heard the Woman calling her. She got up from the floor and moved closer to the opening of the shed and looked through fine, misty rain toward the house. The Woman was standing in the kitchen door, drawing through her hands a long, wicked-looking switch, an expression of evil glee upon her face.

She's looking forward to lashing me, enjoying the very notion of it, Deborah thought with a kind of wondering horror. She drew quickly back from the opening and wriggled her slim body into the narrow space between the stacked wood and the wall of the shed. The Woman's voice still calling her name, softly now and pretending sweetness as if she would show that she had forgiven Deborah, came nearer. The Woman came to the very entrance of the shed and peered in. Deborah pressed against the wall, holding her breath to make herself as small as she could, willing the Woman to go away. After a moment the fat figure waddled off into the yard, muttering, "Drat the varmint. Where'd she get to?"

Deborah stayed in her crack until she judged it safe again, then went cautiously to the opening and, standing as much as she could in the deep shadow, set herself to watch. In a few minutes she heard the kitchen door slam and saw the Woman, bonneted and shawled, come out and take the back path that led to the house of her crony, Mistress Patch.

When she was out of sight, Deborah ran to the house and let herself in, easing the door shut behind her. There was no more time to plan. She must get out of here at once and do her thinking later.

A half-loaf of bread was on the table and beside it part of a chicken. She took them and remembered to fill an old leathern flask of Uncle Matt's with water from the wooden bucket under the window. Hurrying, she went up the crooked stair that led to the small room at the top of the house which had been hers for seven years. She took her few clothes from the hooks and chest, made them into a bundle with the food in the middle in a length of old linen cloth that had come marred from the loom. She covered the whole thing in her shawl, started for the stairs, remembered she would not, the Lord being willing, ever come back here, and went back for her long winter cloak.

She took a final look about the room, saw the comb and the scrap of mirror Uncle Matt had given her, still in their places on the pine table, and put them in her pocket. Sure she was ready now, she closed the door behind her and went down the stairs and out into the street.

A light drizzle of rain was still falling and she was glad of the woolen cloak, hot though it was, for it kept out the damp. She set her back to the leaden strip of the river that ran by the foot of the lot and started toward the center of the town. The afternoon was waning. Before long it would be getting dark. She must think of somewhere to spend the night, somewhere she'd be safe from the Watch, somewhere dry where she could have a little uninterrupted while to try to solve her problems.

She had been walking aimlessly, her only thought to put as much space between herself and the Woman as fast as she could. Where had she got to? She stopped and looked ahead and saw the State House. It stood, foursquare, solid, somehow comforting in its mass and dignity. Her eyes lifted to the top where a weather vane showed the wind northwesterly. Beneath the weather vane in its own housing was the State House bell rung to announce the meetings of the Assembly or the Courts of Justice. The "Liberty Bell" people had named it since it had sent its joyous peal out and out across the land when the members of the Continental Congress had at last signed the declaration that broke the political ties, please God forever, between the American colonies and England.

Liberty Bell. Why shouldn't it provide her with the liberty she was seeking, the liberty to think her way through her problems—at least for tonight? She could get to it. She knew the way, remembered it clearly from the day two years ago when Uncle Matt had taken her with him to watch his friend Andrew McNair muffle and toll it because the ships bearing the hated tax stamps from London were coming into the port of Philadelphia. The little house that sheltered the bell would shelter her. There was room to stretch out on the plank flooring and she would be quite safe because no one came to the bell tower except for a ringing.

"Come then, Deborah Stone," she said aloud to herself, "why are you dawdling? Best get up and settled before the dark comes down."

She took a firmer grip on her bundle and went, almost running, to the door she knew of that would take her to shelter and safety for the night.

A lantern burning dimly at the foot of the tower stairs and another halfway up gave enough light in the shadowy place to show her the way. When she reached the top, out of breath and a little dizzy, she found that the drizzle had stopped at least for the time. It was dark now but the cloud scud showed here and there a few pale stars and, briefly, the horn of the new moon. She set her bundle on the floor and went to stand beneath the huge, inverted metal cup. By reaching on tiptoe she could just manage to trace the words on its rim:

Proclaim liberty throughout all the land, unto all the inhabitants thereof

and she felt again the tingle of excitement she'd known when first Uncle Matt had read out that prophetic message.

Her mind lifted with the realization that she was, herself, free. Free of the Woman. Free to come and go as she would. Free to try to find an active place for herself in the fight. She'd heard from Uncle Matt stories of spies—of John and Jacob Levering and Old Mom Rinker who managed somehow to bring bits of tales of Tory infamies to the General. Maybe she could find them and, somehow, become a part of the General's spy ring. There'd likely be danger in it, but what did she care for danger of that sort? It was only the Woman she feared now.

Suddenly she was conscious of tiredness—all the way to her bones—and hunger. She sat beside her bundle and opened it and took out her stolen food and ate half the chicken and a piece of bread, washing them down with water from the flask. She barely had energy enough to do up the bundle again before she stretched on the boards and pulled her cloak around her against the chill of the September night.

She lay there awhile, watching the stars appear and disappear as the scarf of clouds was blown about the dark vault of the sky by a brisk wind. She was not afraid of the dark. It wrapped her in comfort. She could see the blacker shadow of the bell swinging a very little on its beam. "Proclaim liberty." That was a good thing, she thought drowsily, and heard again in memory Colonel John Nixon's strong, clear voice reading solemnly the words of the Declaration, "When in the course of human events it becomes necessary"; heard again the jubilant ringing out of liberty; saw in memory the flare of bonfires lighted to honor the new light of freedom on the eighth day of July—over a year ago now. She wondered where Uncle Matt was this night and, wondering, shut her eyes and drifted into sleep.

CHAPTER FIVE

She was awakened by the dawn singing of the birds. She reached up to trace once more the message on the bell and heard, with joy, as if at a good omen, a small answering ring from the metal. The air was clear and sparkling, and she took a dancing step or two, her spirits lifting with the lifting sun. What had she to do with despair? She was strong, tall enough to pass for seventeen, willing to work and able to learn. She would find ways to keep herself. She would go from big house to big house until she came upon one in need of a serving maid.

She took her bundle and groped her way down the stairs, dark now that the candles in the lanterns had sputtered out. The silent, empty streets reminded her she must wait upon the eating of breakfasts and the start of the day's household chores. It could not yet be six o'clock and city folk, certainly those rich enough to hire serving maids, would not be up as yet. Never mind. She would go to Bathsheba's Bath and Bower and wash her face in its still, cool spring and break her own fast in comfort beside its quiet waters.

It was good to be alive, to be free of the Woman, to be starting an adventure all her own. If only she were a boy and could be going to General George

Washington's headquarters to join Uncle Matt as a soldier! It wasn't fair that girls had to sit at home and wonder while the men took their guns and fought for the freedom they so well believed must come. Drat! She just wouldn't think of that now.

She turned into Second Street and saw the Bath and Bower ahead of her, still and silent in the emptiness of its unawakened world. She knelt beside the spring and cupped water in her hands and dashed it into her face and mouth.

People were passing now in the street and looking at her curiously, but it was still too early to knock at the door of any of the elegant houses that lined the street. For an hour then she went about the streets, seeing the houses and the neat, bright shops with a fresh eye as if she were newly come to the town. As always, as she walked, she looked for the boy, Johnny Darragh, but she did not see him.

By the time she approached the first white, paneled door with the big brass knocker that must have come from England, she had lost her confidence and was ready to turn and run away. But she spoke sternly to herself and forced herself to raise the knocker and let it fall again; once, twice, a third time. She fancied she could hear the sound reverberating inside, in waves that diminished in strength and overlapped like an echo. Her uneasiness urged her to run and run, now before it was too late.

She rooted her feet to the brick path and tried to forget panic by counting. She had reached eighty when the door opened, so silently that she jumped though she had indeed expected it to open some time.

A girl stood in the doorway, a girl not much older than she but with a discontented expression and a superior air. A close, white cap sat stiffly upon curls Deborah was sure had been made by sleeping with her head wrapped in rags. A gray linsey-woolsey dress fell almost to the tops of neat black slippers and was partly covered by a starched white apron. The girl stood there, staring, saying nothing while Deborah gulped and could pick no proper words from the muddle in her mind.

"Well," the girl said at last, disagreeably, "what do you want?" She sounded impatient and cross and managed to give the simple words the color of an insult.

"I—I"—Deborah gulped desperately again and then forced herself to go on—"I'm looking for work. Do you—"

"Work! Work is it? And have you no more sense than to come knocking at the front door like gentry? You'll not likely find work when it's clear you don't even know enough to go to the back where you belong. Go away. We'd have nothing to do with the likes of you."

She shut the door, none too gently, and Deborah, her face red with shame and anger, ran from the house as quickly as her stumbling legs would take her. That girl, that high-and-mighty, hoity-toity *female* had no cause to treat her like—like trash. The more she thought about it, the angrier she became, and anger made her forget shame and stiffened the purpose she'd been ready a moment ago to abandon. She deliberately chose a house she'd seen some five minutes' walk away. That would give her a little time to calm her roiling thoughts and compose her face, and this time she would go at once, all docile and begging, to the back door.

There was no work at the next house.

At house after house she was turned away, sometimes disdainfully, sometimes courteously. Some places, when she came up to them, were shuttered and barred, and she guessed those had belonged to friends of the patriot cause who had already, with more prudence than courage, expecting the coming of the British, taken themselves and their possessions out of Philadelphia where they would be safer.

By midday the morning's coolness had been swallowed up in damp heat. Her bundle, and the heavy cloak, long since folded across her arm, seemed unbelievably heavy. She was hungry and thirsty and tired and discouraged. There was only one house remaining on her mind's list and it was the least promising.

She went to it timidly and as timidly knocked on the door that stood open as if it would invite any vagrant air that might be stirring. She could hear sounds of movement from the shadowy room. The smell of meat cooking made her feel faint, remembering the dreary hours since she'd eaten her breakfast. She leaned against the doorjamb while a long, long minute went by with no answer to her knock. She was about to try again when a voice called, "Come along in then," and she half-fell through the door.

A big, rosy-faced woman was tending a joint of meat, basting it with a long-handled spoon full of a sauce that smelled faintly of mint. She finished the basting and turned from the fire so quickly Deborah hadn't time to rearrange her face that had been yearning toward the food.

"Bless my soul," the woman said, "you're hungry by the looks of you. Sit down there by the table and I'll find you a bite of something."

"Th-thank you," Deborah said, ready to cry at the first real kindness she'd met this day.

When food was set before her she ate with gusto, finished the last crumb and, secretly, licked her fingers. A long sigh of satisfaction trailed from her before she could stop it and upon that the woman turned and said, "Well now. You do look less famished. Had you something in your mind beyond food when you came knocking at my kitchen door?"

"Yes, Mistress. But first thank you. Thank you for food that was sorely needed."

"No call for thanks. Now what would you be asking me?"

Deborah smiled. "Another favor like enough. Would you need a—a serving maid, or help here in your kitchen? I've come from Lancaster way. (Deborah thought there was no need to add her coming had been seven years ago!) I'm looking for work to keep me here in the town."

"You've come to a poor place then. My people are none so rich they can be hiring a whole parcel of helpers. But stay now, child. No need to look so downhearted. It's not the end of the world."

"I've tried and I've tried," Deborah said forlornly, "and there's just—nothing." She wanted, suddenly, to put her head on this kind woman's shoulder and blurt out her whole true story but she shut her lips tightly, reminding herself she had no assurance she wouldn't be sent back where she'd come from. Whatever happened she was *not* going to return to the Woman. If the worst came she could find something to work at out Germantown way maybe. And that would, at least, be on the other side of town from the Woman and her Uncle Cyrus.

"Wait now," her companion was saying, "all's not lost. I heard in the street, they do be needing a kitchen maid at the Four Alls."

"The—Four—Alls?"

"It's a tavern, mind, but a decent one. Takes its name from the sign that reads,

> KING—I govern all
> GENERAL—I fight for all
> MINISTER—I pray for all
> LABORER—And I pay for all

The tavern's kept by some people named—now what was that name? Ford? Yes, Ford it is. Betsy and Jeremiah Ford. Might be they've found nobody yet and will take you on. But it will be hard work, child, hard work and long hours."

Deborah was already on her way to the door. "I'm not afraid of work," she said and thanked her benefactor again and fervently.

She remembered seeing that sign this very morning, remembered the pictures of King, General, Clergyman and Laborer. She would hurry, and pray as she went that the Fords had not found a replacement for their lost help.

She hardly noticed the heat and the weight of her bundles as she moved once more through the steamy streets. She was confident again, forgetful of the disappointments of the day. She found the Inn and the kitchen door down a short lane and noticed with pleasure the tall trees and grass that bordered the paved courtyard outside it. She rapped and a thin woman with a flushed face and a harried look answered her knock.

"I'm looking for Mistress Ford," Deborah said.

The woman wiped her face where the sweat from the hot day and the hot stove within was making rivulets along the sallow skin of a person who seldom gets out in the sunlight. "I'm Mistress Ford," she said, "and I would thank you to say quickly what you want of me, for I'm shorthanded and hurried."

"I heard you need a kitchen maid—" Deborah began, and got no further with the story she'd prepared to account for herself and her need for work. Mistress Ford took her arm and fairly pulled her through the door.

"Come in, come in. Welcome as Christmas you are if so be you're offering yourself for hiring." Deborah nodded and Mistress Ford went on, "Pure answer to prayer. I've been that troubled and rushed since I had to send that girl away when I caught her stealing. *You* won't steal, will you? Indeed you do have an honest look about you." She stopped, out of breath, and Deborah said, quietly, reassuringly, "No, Mistress, I'll not steal if so be you're willing to hire me."

47

"*Hire* you! Willing to hire you? You're hired already, girl. What *is* your name now?"

"Deborah Stone." She wondered if she should have given another name because of the Woman and reassured herself again that the Woman would hardly come looking for her. No matter in any case. What was done was done and no need to waste worry on it.

"Then come you in, Deborah Stone. Put your things in yonder cupboard and start to work this minute. The Lord knows I can use you. Later, I'll show you your room abovestairs. Now there's bread to be cut and the table to be set for dinner for half a dozen hungry travelers arrived unexpectedly and all the more welcome since few come from afar since the war."

Deborah was too busy for the next few hours helping to serve the travelers, washing the dishes, scouring pots and pans until their tin surfaces gleamed, to think about her good fortune, though she found a moment to be grateful to the Woman, for once, for the hours of harsh training in the myriad tasks of a well-kept house. It was nearly sundown when the kitchen and dining room were finally set to rights and Mistress Ford turned to her with a smile that, though tired, was pleased.

"You'll do, Deborah," she said, and Deborah felt her face burn with pleasure at the sparse but heartfelt praise. "Now if you'll get your cloak and bundle I'll show you your room and you'll have time for a bit of rest before supper."

She led Deborah up two flights of stairs.

"It's a lovely room, Mistress," Deborah said.

"But I'd best tell you straight out," Mistress Ford said,

"though the telling may lose me your help, there's no promising how long we'll be staying."

"Staying?" Deborah asked, sounding as puzzled as she felt.

"It's the British. They do be saying all over the town the British will come. When they do—*if* they do, for my Jeremiah thinks it likely General Washington will whip Howe's men as he whipped the other redcoats at Trenton last Christmas—if the British come we'll be bound to leave."

"But—but why?" Deborah was trying hard to hold to her new-found security. "Won't the British gentlemen drink punch?"

"Not from the likes of us." Mistress Ford hesitated so long Deborah thought she wasn't going on but at last she gave a kind of grudging nod and spoke again. "My husband and I are heart and soul for General Washington and a free country; dead set against the wicked George in London, may the devil fly away with him. Our place here—well, the gentlemen you've seen below are patriots all. They come here to think and plan how to help the Continental Army as I don't doubt they're doing at this minute. Do you think, then, we'll be waiting for the British to enter the city—for there's plenty willing to tell General Howe or General Cornwallis or another how we've harbored the enemies of the king—and take us away to one of their stinking prison ships? We'll stay as long as we can but when we hear the redcoats are heading for Philadelphia for sure, we'll be on our way within the hour to a place we'll be safe. Now, if you've a mind that loves the British—and there's many such hereabouts and a pox upon them—you'd best be leaving."

Deborah thought scornfully that this Mistress Ford and her husband were indeed cowards. *She* wouldn't run away because the British were coming. Maybe, if they did come; maybe *then* she would find her chance to spy—all by herself if she couldn't manage to join Old Mom Rinker or the Levering boys or somebody else. Never mind for now. The Fords were not Tories anyway and she had found sanctuary. "I'll be staying, Mistress Ford. I'm no king-lover. My uncle—he's all the family I've got now—has gone for a soldier with General Washington and I would surely have gone with him if I'd only been a boy. It's more than likely your husband is right and General Washington will whip the redcoats before they can come to the city. Meantime it will be a pleasure to help serve the patriot gentlemen."

The frown at last left Mistress Ford's face. She caught Deborah in a great hug and said, "It's settled then. Do you dispose your things and we'll have such another supper as will make us forget the British and all their evil works for a little time at least."

CHAPTER SIX

The next fortnight went so quickly Deborah wondered what had become of the minutes and hours and days. She fell easily into the routine of work at the Four Alls. She made the beds in the rooms reserved for travelers, polished the furniture and pewter until they shone with a silken patina, helped Mistress Ford prepare the dwindling supply of food, agreeing inside herself when Jeremiah cursed the war-frightened people with money to spend who were buying great quantities of staples and storing them against what the gentlemen who came each evening for punch and talk were predicting would be a lean winter.

The gentlemen forgathered now about an applewood fire to keep out the chill of September evenings. Deborah, moving among them as quietly as the shadow of a leaf, listened to bits and pieces of their talk as she served them. She felt a kind of excitement that she was part of this new burgeoning of liberty. And again she wished she hadn't been born a girl.

Each night the number of gentlemen who came regularly to the tavern was smaller. One by one they were closing their shops and their countinghouses and leaving the town. The Tories looked forward to the coming of the British. They remained. And the people, largely Quakers, who were against any fighting remained. And, Jeremiah said sourly, managed to keep their affairs flourishing. But none of these men frequented the tavern which had a name as a resort for patriots.

Deborah shivered whenever the gentlemen talked of the whereabouts of General Howe, who was moving toward Philadelphia with seventeen thousand British and Hessian troops. She tried to hold to her belief that General Washington would stop them, but she found it hard to do when the gentlemen were so pessimistic.

There was little to break the comforting monotony

of each day's work. Once Deborah and Mistress Ford went out into the street but they saw nothing except a line of carriages and wagons filled with men in the sober clothes of the Society of Friends. The line moved slowly, to the music of fifes and drums, escorted by members of the City Guard toward the Wilmington Road. The faces of the men were sad or angry and Mistress Ford explained in answer to Deborah's questions these were the Quaker exiles being sent to Virginia because they had been suspected of giving information to the British and had refused to promise not to do so in the future. Deborah remembered the frenzied face of the tall boy who had urged his friends to throw Johnny Darragh into the river and thought his uncle must be in one of the wagons.

Then on September 11 word came that Washington's army had been defeated at Brandywine. Deborah thought achingly of Uncle Matt until her heart was near to breaking.

When she heard that all the bells in the town were to be taken from their mountings and sent to a place where the British could not steal them and melt them for bullets, she begged for a free hour. She wanted to say a silent fare-you-well to *her* bell.

She stood with a small group of loiterers and watched men lower the Liberty Bell from its housing. It looked somehow forlorn when it was, at last, standing in the street, its metal dead and useless, its ringing stilled. As men swathed it in packing and lifted it to a waiting wagon she listened to the talk around her. The wagon would join a supply train of seven hundred others taking the heavy baggage of the

Continental Army to Allentown. All the bells of Philadelphia's churches would go in the train, guarded by two hundred cavalrymen from North Carolina and Virginia. The bells would stay, swaddled and muffled but safe, in Allentown until the British were driven out of the City of Brotherly Love.

"Brotherly Love," indeed, Deborah thought, remembering the hating looks and words that had passed between Tories and patriots these two years past, the cannon ready for firing, the small boats withdrawn from their customary peaceful uses for business and pleasure and hurried across the Delaware so the British would get no advantage from them. Her mind felt dull and heavy with the burden of war and waiting and wondering when she would be alone again. And what would she do then?

She forced the thoughts from her mind. The great bell was in its place now in the wagon. She wished she could once more run her fingers around its rim, feeling the message of liberty raised there, and started for the Four Alls. She wished she had not watched this sad dismantling of what she had come to think of as a living thing, wished she had not to go home through streets that seemed unfriendly and brooding with the Bell gone. As she turned, her eye caught a familiar tall figure with a scowling face at the edge of the crowd and she recognized the leader of the gang of boys who had tormented Johnny Darragh. It was almost as if her thought of him a week ago had called him to her, and she shivered. He had not seen her and she dodged behind the broad backs of two dockhands who had stopped to watch. She had no wish to tangle with that boy again and, as soon as she

could, she ducked into an alleyway where she was hidden from any glance he might send toward her. She had no liking for his kind of cruelty and bullying. Indeed, she admitted to herself with shame, she was more than a little frightened of him.

Was it not strange, she thought, that she should find him upon whom she would have been just as happy never to set eyes when she could not find the other boy from that day in the alley? But she *would* find him some day. And then maybe they could, together, work out a way to serve the General. She sighed. First she'd have to find Johnny Darragh and her work for Mistress Ford left her few chances to look. Why couldn't it have been Johnny watching the departure of the Bell?

As she hurried down the alley she wondered who

the tall, mean one was and where he lived, and
hoped she'd not come upon him again. When the
alley came to an end she made her way by back
streets to the tavern.

The word she had been dreading to hear came on
the night of the twenty-fourth of September. Mistress
Ford waited until supper was over and the kitchen
was made neat and ready for the next day. Jeremiah
had gone from habit to the taproom though it had
been empty these last two nights since his final
customers had fled for safety beyond the city. Mistress
Ford turned from the ashes she'd been raking carefully
to the back of the fireplace and, not looking at
Deborah, said, "Tomorrow before sunup so none will
know of it, we go."

Deborah said, "Oh." The word made a small, empty sound in the quiet room reflecting the emptiness in her mind which was all she could feel now she was faced with the dreaded thing she'd pushed determinedly from her thinking during most of the past three weeks.

"I wish we could take you with us, child." Mistress Ford sounded distressed as she came to Deborah and put an arm about the drooping shoulders. "I would if I could for I've come to be right fond of you and that's a fact. I've thought and thought to find a way but there is none. My sister will take us in, being blood kin and obligated, but she's none too cheerful about it for she has but little room to spare. Her own family is large and the two of us, just the two of us, will crowd her small house. There's no room for a third. And we dare not leave this place open for the British to ransack as they please, else you could stay on here until you've found settlement elsewhere. There's but one thing I've thought of. The stable is clean and empty and Jeremiah's spread fresh hay in the loft. You'll be safe enough there and warm and we'll leave you what food there is—enough to keep you from hunger for a few days. I—I'm sorry," she finished lamely and Deborah nodded and said, "I do understand, Mistress. I'll—I'll manage," and went for the last time to the room that had been her sanctuary.

She slept very little, if indeed she slept at all. But wakefulness brought no answer to the question that seemed to grow bigger and bigger with the piling of hour upon dark hour until she felt smothered by it.

She had now no thought or recollection of thought

of working for the Cause; no courage to spin dreams of what she could do if only she were a boy or could find some member of the General's spy ring. Now her whole being was centered hopelessly, helplessly upon two questions.

What could she do now?

Where could she go?

She told herself, sternly, to stop worrying and think, plan, dream something upon which she could act tomorrow. But worry stayed uppermost in her, a glue that thickened her brain and forbade intelligent thinking.

At first light she got up and dressed and remade the bundle she'd opened so gladly only three weeks ago. She made the room neat and went, dull-eyed and dull-witted, down the two flights of steps.

Neither she nor Mistress Ford could find words as they went about collecting bread and cheese and what remained of the joint of stringy beef they had eaten yesterday. Deborah took the food and the bundle of her belongings to the stable and climbed the steep ladder to the haymow and laid the two packages in the hay that still carried, faintly, the smell of summer's warmth.

She did not think. She could not feel anything. She pinched her own arm, hard, and noticed no pain.

The gray day was wrapped in stillness as the Fords silently mounted their borrowed horses. Mistress Ford, at the last moment, went to the post where the tavern sign swung lightly, creaking a little. She slipped the sign from its hooks and, holding it clumsily under one arm, put her foot into her husband's hands and was

lifted onto the pillion. She arranged her cloak carefully and, as Jeremiah mounted the other horse, leaned
down and laid her hand briefly against Deborah's
cheek in a parting caress. She tried to speak and
could not and turned her head sharply away. Jeremiah
said, "Gee-*up*," and the horses ambled out onto the
cobbled pavement.

Deborah stood a minute or two in the gloomy
morning, watching them, then turned and walked to
the stable and climbed the ladder again and lay down
upon the hay, gathering her cloak about her to keep
out the early fall damp. Winter, she thought, winter
isn't far off and what will become of me then? She
wished she could cry away the weight that lay like a
physical thing upon her mind and heart but no tears
would come. She lay for a long time, looking at the
rafter beams above her. After a while she closed her
eyes against the emptiness of her mind and slipped,
without knowing it, into the sleep her tired body
craved.

She awoke, hours later, hearing at a little distance
the normal sounds of the city; street calls, the thud
of feet on cobblestones, a horse clopping along.

She was exhausted but the ice about her mind had,
at last, broken and she could think. She knew she must
not stay here in the city, unfriended, with only the
pittance she had earned as wages to buy necessary
food and shelter. And she couldn't go back to the
Woman! She must, somehow, get out of Philadelphia,
find General Washington's headquarters and Uncle
Matt. He would tell her what to do. Maybe she could
stay on with him, be one of the women who, she had

heard, followed their husbands and fathers and sweethearts even into battle and brought them water.

She had only a vague idea where Washington's men were camped. She knew she must go toward Germantown. That would do for a start. Once outside the town she could ask the way. She would not go until tomorrow. For the rest of the day she would stay here where she was warm and dry.

CHAPTER SEVEN

The noon-high sun was hot on the shadeless roadside where Deborah sat the next day. She had gotten up early, her mind alert and relieved because she had slept soundly once she had decided to find Uncle Matt—or try to. But the morning had been difficult and long and hope had waned with its passing.

She had thought there was no one left in Philadelphia except British-lovers and neutrals but the streets were already alive with escaping people, a few in carts, the majority on foot carrying such possessions as they could in packs on their shoulders or in their hands. Yesterday, while Deborah was too sunk in her numbness to hear or heed it, word had come that Lord Cornwallis would march today into the city of Philadelphia at the head of a large part of General Howe's army and would hold it for the British Crown. Cornwallis had promised, so the people had been told, that no one would be molested so long as they behaved quietly and submitted without objection to the decrees of the generals. But few patriots believed him and those who had been unwilling to think the enemy would actually take the town and, therefore, slow to leave it had worked frantically through the day and night to prepare for last-minute flight.

By the time Deborah left the courtyard of the Four Alls there were, in the streets, two thin streams of people, some headed toward the crossings of the Delaware River, others going in the opposite direction. Babies were crying. Toddlers walked with frightened eyes, holding to their mothers' dresses. Older children tried to look as if they were not as afraid as their younger brothers and sisters. There was no sound of voices except when a woman hushed a child or a man grunted softly to a horse or dog.

Deborah had joined the stream going toward the Germantown Road. She had made no attempt to speak to any of the others, her heart distressed at the sight of the pitiful piles of belongings each family hoped to save. The going was slow and became slower when the refugees began to meet the first elements of Lord Cornwallis' army. As she watched the ranks of smart soldiers—the clean red-coated British Grenadiers and Guards, the tall-hatted and sour-faced Hessians, the lines of bristling cannon swinging in precise rhythm, rank upon close and orderly rank—Deborah began for the first time to fear for the success of this war for liberty to which she was committed in her heart. She remembered the scornful Tory comments when George Washington had paraded his tatterdemalions through Philadelphia, only a month ago. Would all the battles to be fought end as Brandywine had ended? Then she heard in memory Uncle Matt's stout defense of the Continentals and recalled how he had once said that belief in an honest cause was worth a regiment of hirelings, and she stiffened her courage.

The oncoming soldiers did not harry the refugees. They had hardly a glance for that other small, poor army they were passing. But the British came on, relentlessly, never breaking step, down the road, and the escaping families were forced again and again to scurry to the roadside and wait until a column had passed.

By noon they had come only a mile or two beyond the town. There were, then, no more British to delay them but Deborah's legs ached and her arms felt too tired to carry her bundle one step further. She had to rest awhile and she went to the roadside and dropped onto a little grassy bank to recuperate her spirit and her body.

How was she ever going to find Uncle Matt? She had stopped a peddler going toward Philadelphia with his pack of needles and thread, pins and patches, wondering that he should still be walking the roads at such a time. She had asked him for news of Washington's headquarters but he had only shaken his head and gone on his hurrying way resentful of the small moment of time lost by her query. Once, too, she had gathered courage to put her question to one of the men traveling near her. He had not, she thought, even heard her, so lost was he in his own troubles, and she had not asked again.

She rubbed her legs and stared after the last of the refugees filling the road ahead, growing smaller each moment. She was too tired and too dispirited to follow them now. She would sit here awhile longer before she tried to find a house where she could once more ask her way.

A patch of song started her out of torpor. It was a lilting, marching song she knew so well she was saying the words in her mind before she fully realized she was hearing the tune:

> Through the woods we go
> And through the boggy mire
> Straightway till we come to our hearts' desire.
> Oh dooley, dooley day
> Oh the little dooley day.

Uncle Matt had taught her the song. It was, he had said, a song the Continental soldiers were singing—sadly and slowly about their campfires at night; quickly, with spirit as they marched to battle.

The words finished in her head and, at the same moment, she saw the singer as he emerged from the screen of the retreating refugee column. He was swinging along the road in time to his music as if there were no war, no care in all the world. He was carrying a filled sack. It must be heavy from the size of it, but its weight seemed to rest as easily as a feather upon his shoulder as he balanced it with one hand, the other swinging in time with his song. She knew him at once; knew him with a lightening of her heart, a lifting of her spirits that had no basis in reason but that, nevertheless, brought a ghost smile to her eyes. Johnny Darragh, whom she'd looked for without success wherever she'd been in the streets of the city, was singing along this doleful road. He was so different today, so

blithe and bonny and joyful, he seemed another person altogether. Even his clothes, gray and powdered as were hers with road dust, seemed somehow less somber.

He saw her and swerved from the middle of the road and came to stand above her. He looked down into her face and she saw, at once, he recognized her too. He lowered his sack carefully to the grass and followed it to sit beside her.

"Good day, Mistress," he said. "And a very good day it is since it brings me at last to thee. Does thee know I've been searching the face of each lady I've seen this past month till I was like to have the Watch set upon me for prying, hoping to find thee?" His face and half-teasing voice sobered as he went on. "Indeed I have wanted each day to thank thee for my life and to bring thee to my mother and father so they too could thank thee. The dear knows what I would have done if thee had not come to aid me. For in truth I had no notion but that day would be my last."

She said, embarrassed, "Please. I don't want any thanks. It was nothing I did, nothing anyone wouldn't have done."

"Still I thank thee," he said, "and it was a deal more than nothing. It was a stout thing."

She fidgeted, distressed and tongue-tied by his thanks. He seemed to sense her discomfiture and spoke again to relieve it. "What is it brings thee here to the roadside with thy goods and chattels about thee?" He pointed to her bundle. She thought he had a strange way of speaking, almost like a schoolmaster.

She told him, then, in a rush, not waiting to count the cost, because she must tell someone, the whole of

64

her story. He listened without a word, though she was a time in the telling, until she was done. Then he shook his head, his face solemn.

"I can tell thee the road to General Washington's headquarters for I have often been there to visit my brother," he said, "but I doubt it would be anyways sensible for thee to seek out the army."

"Not sensible? How else can I find my uncle?"

"Look thee, Mistress. . . ." He stopped and stared at her and laughed. "Now here is a thing!" he went on. "Thee saved my very life and I know all about thee— or a deal of it—but do I know thy name? I do not. Tell it me and it please thee, for sure and I cannot go on calling thee Mistress forever."

"Deborah Stone," she said and surprised herself by fetching the shadow of a smile at the look on his face.

"Then see now, Deborah Stone. There's no assurance thy uncle will be at the headquarters."

"But he said he was going there to join General Washington. Where else . . . ?"

He held up two fingers to stop her. "That was a full month ago. Likely he did go to the General. But that's not to say he's still there. There's more than one part to our Continental Army and every man is sent where he is most needed. He might be in Jersey or York State or at one of the forts in the Delaware that will be trying to starve out the British by keeping old Howe's brother from bringing his supply ships upriver. There's no saying where 'Uncle Matt' is and even General Washington's army is no place for a girl without a protector."

"Oh!" Deborah said. Her first reaction was to the

last of his talk. There it was again. A girl was no good, nothing but a trouble and a nuisance in war. Then full understanding came to her and she said in so small a voice he could hardly hear it, "Then what's to become of me? What can I do?"

He laughed at her woebegone expression. "Come home with me," he said, as if that were the most natural thing in the world.

"Home with you?" She was repeating his words like a talking parrot she'd once seen on the shoulder of a sailing man new come to port from Jamaica but her mind seemed incapable of taking in what her ears were hearing.

"Stop your aping of me, Goose," he said, but the quality of his voice showed he was not angry, only teasing, "and *listen*."

"Yes." She tried to recall the smile to show him she understood the teasing, and could not.

"Best I tell a mite about us Darraghs," Johnny went on, "since likely thee be wondering how a family like us with a member in the Continental Army dares stay the coming of the redcoats and if it be safe to stay with us."

Deborah nodded. She would indeed have been wondering just that if she'd had any space in her mind for curiosity.

"There be two reasons likely. The one, we're Friends and the British think all Friends are friends to them." He grinned again at his own play on words. "The other, my mother and father are Irish-born and -bred. Came to Philadelphia, they did, after they were wed. And my mother's cousin, Captain Barrington, is with General

Howe himself which news he sent my mother in a letter from New York when first the British came. So we figure we're safe enough, if we're careful to watch our tongues. And thee'll be safe enough with us."

"But, your mother? Your whole family? How can I just come and—and sit down on you?"

"Goose! There's room to spare in the Loxley House where we live and thee'll be made right welcome. Likely my mother will find plenty for thee to do so thee'll not feel a burden, though there's no call to be beholden to us in any way, mind. My mother's forever complaining she and my older sister have no more than four hands and four feet between them. Will thee come then—*at least* until we can find out about Uncle Matt?"

For a moment Deborah couldn't speak, so great was her relief. To her dismay she felt her eyes wet, and rubbed them with her knuckles to send the tears away. When she judged she could speak steadily she said, "Right gladly and I thank you."

"No thanks needed," he said, and got up and took his sack, explaining he'd been to the mill and the sack was full of flour. He would have taken her bundle as well but she wouldn't let him.

"I thought it weighed a hundredweight when I sat here," she said, "but I reckon it was more likely not knowing what I was going to do that was the burden. Now—now this carries itself and seems as light as a bee resting on a flower."

He started his song again as they moved into the empty road and this time she joined in. Their two voices, both clear and sweet, blended well and in a bare thirty minutes they had covered the space it had taken four hours to cover earlier and were again in Philadelphia.

Deborah scarcely could believe the change that had taken place in the city in the short time since she had left it. There was a sense of excitement and bustle, almost of gaiety, everywhere. Shops which had not already been boarded up and left by their patriot owners were closed as for a holiday. Many of them showed the British flag in windows or upon staffs on their roofs. Men and women in their best clothes strolled about the streets, smiling and chatting. Here and there a British officer, splendid in immaculate white breeches and scarlet coat, went purposefully, acknowledging the greetings of the Tories with supercilious nods. A regiment of black-uniformed Hessian fusiliers, hirelings of King George, marching smartly to fife and drum, passed on their way to their quarters. Small boys with sticks on their shoulders marched beside them pretending to be soldiers but the Hessians kept their eyes straight ahead and took no heed of the joyous children. The mouths of the soldiers turned down as if to show their drooping spirits and, for a moment, Deborah felt sorry for them. She had heard it said they were miserable, homesick in this land so far away from the green forests of their native Germany, whose customs were strange and whose language they couldn't understand. Then the brief inclination to pity was swept away in anger at the city that welcomed an invading army as if it were no more than a traveling puppet show come to bring them pleasure.

She started to speak her thoughts but Johnny Darragh stopped her quickly. "Say nothing," he whispered.

68

"Don't even *think* about them. From this moment thee must guard thyself whenever thee walks abroad so no one will guess thee is a patriot. We will all be in danger—all those patriots left—for the British will suspect us all of helping the General and will be too ready to seize us and take us to the hulks as prisoners."

She looked at him curiously. Why was he so afraid of the British? For the intensity of his words went beyond ordinary caution. She thought the British general would be foolish to fill his prison ships with ordinary people, women and children and old men who weren't able to do anything really to harm their enemies no matter how much they would like to. What had the British to fear from such as she, for example, who couldn't even dream reasonably about aiding her cause? Surely even the British would not expect to be loved and welcomed by people like the Darraghs whose sons or husbands or sweethearts were fighting for the right to live free of English tyranny. Whatever was the matter with Johnny? Was he daft? She lifted her shoulders and wondered whether she *could* keep her true feelings hidden—or whether she wanted to. Now that the problem of food and shelter was solved, or about to be, she was, once more, zealous to have a part in this war. Maybe she would have been better off if she had stuck to her resolve to find Uncle Matt. "Stupid," she cautioned herself, "you just keep remembering how you felt when you were sitting beside the road before Johnny came. Think of somebody else you can pretend to be when you walk abroad and act as if you were that somebody and you'll be safe enough."

They had turned into Second Street and passed

Bathsheba's Bath and Bower, deserted now, where Deborah had eaten her first breakfast after she had run from the Woman. She wondered where the Old Cow was and looked over her shoulder as if she expected her to appear, shrieking, to grab her. There was, of course, no sign of the discontented face among the people in the street. Deborah had not really thought to see her. The Woman seldom ventured far from the house by the river. Nonetheless, Deborah moved closer to Johnny until she could feel the cloth of his white linen shirt against her arm.

"Here we are then," he said a minute later, breaking the silence that had walked with them since his cautioning.

Deborah looked at the house before them. It seemed a comfortable place, large and roomy with a second-story balcony protected from sun and rain by a roof and marked by a graceful curve. That would be a fine place to watch the street without being noticed should you want to do so. She had no time to count the many windows which, she thought, would make the rooms light in winter and airy in summer, before Johnny was opening the door and inviting her in.

A pleasant voice greeted the opening door. "Is that thee, Johnny? Thee's been overlong. I was beginning to fear—"

Johnny called quickly; almost, Deborah thought, as if he were warning the speaker against finishing what she had started; "I've brought thee company, Ma. Come and make her welcome."

Deborah thought she heard a little gasp before

Johnny's mother answered, "Coming," but she couldn't be sure and she forgot about it as a slight, delicate woman in Quaker gray came toward them. Her complexion was fair. Her hair was light brown, her eyes blue and very bright. Though she had obviously been about her housework she was extremely neat. She looked surprisingly young to have a son in the army.

Johnny said, "Ma, here's the girl I told thee of that helped me the day of the march. Her name's Deborah Stone and she's in a kind of trouble she'll tell thee about herself. I reckon she's in sore need of a friend and I've brought her home to thee. This is my mother, Lydia Darragh, Deborah."

Deborah curtsied and hoped her surprise didn't show. She'd not believed anybody would so confidently bring home a stranger—as he might have brought a stray, lost animal—with no more explanation than Johnny had made. She'll likely send me away, Deborah thought, and prepared to leave quietly and with what dignity she could manage. But Lydia Darragh moved toward her and put an arm about her shoulders and squeezed them hard.

"We do be beholden to thee, Deborah Stone," she said. "And it's glad I am to make thee welcome, as my husband will be glad. We'll talk, if it please thee, of thy trouble later. Thee looks worn out. So now take her upstairs, Johnny, and give the child a chance to rest and refresh herself. Put her in the room next to Susannah's and see there's water in the pitcher. When she's ready there'll be dinner, for I don't doubt both be hungry as titmice."

CHAPTER EIGHT

Deborah thought the time she spent with the Darraghs was, on the whole, the happiest she could remember except for the brief periods when she had been alone with Uncle Matt. She hadn't imagined families could have such fun together; could have such warm and happy times each day.

William Darragh was a quiet, slow-speaking man, a schoolmaster who went his way as if there were no war, or seemed to. He invited Deborah to join his class of Quaker boys and girls and she sat for part of each day listening hard, trying to make up for the seven years when the only learning she had known were the odd half-hours Uncle Matt could spare to teach her to read and write and figure a little. William Darragh was a good teacher and though Deborah took little active part in his classes she learned many things by listening.

She saw little of Johnny's older sister, Ann, a woman grown, who spent a good deal of her time visiting the poor and sick of the Friends' communities or at the Meeting House, to which the other Darraghs went only occasionally. Johnny explained that his mother and father were not altogether welcome since Charles had joined the Continental Army and so preferred to practice their religion at home. Deborah asked if they were not afraid the more orthodox Friends would give away their secret to the British. He smiled a small, wry smile and said that was not the way of the community. There would be no tale-bearing no matter how many heads were shaken in private.

Of the two younger children, eleven-year-old Will was as quiet as his father. He had a passion for the out-of-doors and was off each day as soon as breakfast was done. More often than not he took food with him and didn't come home until near bedtime but no member of the family seemed concerned. "The lad's old enough to take proper care of himself," Lydia said placidly when Deborah ventured to ask about his whereabouts one night. "Best leave him go his own way. He's a good lad and he'll come to no harm."

Susannah, the youngest of Lydia's five living children (four others, Johnny said, had died before he was born) was nine. She was, Deborah thought, a child of light, with hair that shimmered like cornsilk and eyes as blue as her mother's. Susannah seemed never to walk. She moved lightly as a sunbeam and quickly as a breeze on a summer's day, as if indeed she were borne from place to place on invisible wings. She never grumbled, but smiled with quick radiance whenever she looked at you. She took to Deborah at once and followed her wherever she went, becoming Deborah's immediate and well-loved charge—to Lydia's delight. Johnny called the child Deborah's shadow but Deborah only smiled at his teasing for she was well content.

Lydia herself puzzled Deborah somewhat. She moved about her household, outwardly unruffled, but Deborah suspected her of being something more than the gentle, almost feckless soul she seemed. There was a quality of sternness to her eyes, of determination in the very set of her shoulders as she walked that seemed to hint at courage and steadfastness beyond the ordinary. She had, on the first day Deborah had become a member of the household, gently rebuked Deborah for calling her "Mistress," saying that all people were of one nature in the eyes of the Lord and deserved no title that set them apart. It had seemed strange to Deborah, at first, to be calling an older person by her given name but she had become used to it and after the first day or two forgot the strangeness.

At first, Deborah wouldn't leave the house, fearful in spite of herself that she would meet the Woman. Then, a week after she had become a member of the family, Johnny had said, "Why does thee not ever go out into the streets, Deborah? There's much to see."

"Oh,"—Deborah fumbled in her mind for an excuse, not wanting to admit her continuing cowardice—"Oh, there's much to do to help your mother. There's the spinning and weaving and—and the house to keep and . . ."

"And what?" Johnny said as her words trailed off. "Thee's no slavey here, Deborah. Ma *wants* thee to get out. She says thee's pale as a mealy bug that never sees the sun and thee'll sicken for sure if thee stays always within doors."

Deborah wouldn't look at him. She felt she couldn't tell him she was afraid. He'd hate her for being a coward.

"Come on, Deborah. What is it? Something's troubling thee. Tell me."

She hesitated still but she knew she would tell him in the end. Already she had learned Johnny was not one to be put off. He kept looking at her as if he would see right inside her mind to find out her trouble. She felt the blood hot in her face until at last she blurted, not looking at him, "I'm feared I'll meet her I told you of and she'll set the Watch on me to force me back to her. I won't go back."

He did not, at once, comment and she said, miserably, "Now you know. You know I'm—I'm nothing but a coward. I didn't *want* to tell you for you'll likely hate me now."

He took her shoulders. "Goose," he said, "do thee think *I* don't know what it is to be frightened? *Everybody's* frightened sometimes, everybody with sense. But thee can't stay cooped up here forever like a broody hen. I was thinking just now. Thee said she was going out of the city. Already the days are chilly enough for a fire and thee thinks she'd not be one to bring in the wood for herself. Maybe she's already gone. I was thinking I could find out. I could go now. This minute. If she's away thy mind will be free. If she's not . . . well, if she's not we'll tell Ma and she'll think of something. She doesn't hold with any soul being forced to stay with cruel and harsh folk."

He went off before she could argue, before she could even think properly about what he'd been saying. He came back within the hour and the wide smile on his face told her his news before he spoke it. "She's gone right enough," he said. "The house is shuttered and locked. I pretended I had a message from her husband and knocked at a neighbor's door and learned the Woman had left, two days ago, carrying the dear knows how many bundles in a farmer's cart."

For a whole minute Deborah's mind stood still, not yet able to absorb such suddenly-come good fortune. For that minute her body seemed not to be functioning, held in a spell of immobility, her face still set in lines of the fearing unhappiness that had come upon it when Johnny had begun to question her an hour ago. Then the spell broke and she was filled with such a sense of joy she wanted to shout. The Woman was gone; gone the evil spirit that had haunted Deborah Stone daylong and nightlong since she could remember anything clearly. Unconsciously she moved her shoulders as if she were dislodging a heavy physical burden. For as long as the war lasted she would not have to see the Woman again, or fear her. And close upon that thought came another. Likely she need never fear the Woman again, for by the time the war was done she—all of them —would likely be different people from those they had been when it had begun. Better people or worse people but never again the same, for, she was beginning to realize, war did strange things to anyone who was forced to take part in it. And this day another layer of the fears that had begun to go from her when she had stood up to the boys in the alley had been peeled away and she was, therefore, the lighter in spirit.

Johnny, who had been watching her face as ghosts of her thinking moved across it, said, "Does thee feel better now?"

"Yes, oh *yes*. Thank you, Johnny. Thank you. Thank you. And now—now it's time for me to put my whole mind into helping the Cause."

"The Cause?" he repeated as if he thought her daft.

"Certainly the Cause, Goose," she said, trying to read

the expression in his gray eyes. Was it fear? Or something else that made him seem dim-witted? "I know I'm only a girl but there must be *something* I can do—something we can do together, to join the fight even as your brother has joined it. If we go about the city and watch and listen, surely we could find out things—things about the British that would help the General. Nobody would suspect a boy and a girl of—of spying and we could—"

"Hush!" he said harshly. "Thee mustn't say such things. Thee doesn't know what thee is suggesting. Do thee not meddle in things thee doesn't understand."

She stepped back from him, puzzled and hurt by his outburst. "Are you afraid then, Johnny Darragh, to fight in your way for freedom? I had not thought you a coward."

He reached out and took her shoulders and shook her a little. "Does thee call me afraid?" he said, anger making his eyes seem almost black. "Does thee dare . . . ?" He stopped himself in mid-sentence and took back his hands and swallowed once or twice before he spoke again, quietly. "I do beg thy forgiveness, Deborah. I had no call to shout at thee because thee doesn't—doesn't know all I know. But there is danger in what thee would do, great danger of a kind thee cannot know. And I beg thee, never forget thee could do great harm if thee—if thee should meddle."

"Oh!" she said and turned away from him and went to stare out of the window, hurt beyond bearing at his manner and believing no word of what he had said.

"Deborah," he appealed to her back, "Deborah, please," but she didn't turn around. "I'm sorry I

77

angered thee," he went on. "I would tell thee more if—if I could. But I do beg thee, when thee goes about the city, go carefully as if thee walked upon eggs."

Still she wouldn't look at him and after a moment she heard him sigh and go from the room.

For days she saw little of him and could find no time to tell him, once her anger had cooled a little, that she knew she had behaved badly and was sorry. He was, after all, only trying to protect her. She wondered if he were avoiding her or harboring a grudge against her. She didn't think so, for when they met—briefly in the house or at meals—he seemed his natural, buoyant self, laughing, joking, apparently remembering nothing of their quarrel. But he was always going somewhere when they met or else the rest of the family were about and she needed privacy to say what she had to say. An apology was not a thing you wanted to shout out before anybody who chanced to listen. Often and often one of his sentences returned to puzzle and fret her. *"I would tell thee more if I could."* Why had he said that? What did he mean? More about what? Try as she would she could find no answer to those questions and she knew in her heart that even if she could find him alone *he* would give her none.

She had gone freely about the city after that day though she hadn't always enjoyed it. She couldn't get over her first feeling of disgust at the haughty British troops and the fawning pleasure in their presence that showed on the faces of the Tories. Still it was better to be out of the house now and then, as Lydia had said, and she felt the better for her jaunts.

On one of these walks she went to the Square thinking she might climb again to the now empty little house that had once protected "her" bell. She had gone roundabout, for it was a lovely afternoon and she wanted to prolong her delight in the clear air and the blue sky and the sun that warmed her back but did not make her hot. She turned a corner unexpectedly and came upon a single British soldier violently shaking an old, poor-looking man who could evidently do nothing to protect himself. The soldier's face was red and he smelled of the tavern. He was shouting at the old man, "Follow me about, would you? Call me names? Spit upon the King? Dirty, filthy rebel. Happen you be a spy then. Happen I'll take you to my captain and see you strung up by the heels, though hanging's too good for the likes of you. Come along, you!"

Deborah, angry at such behavior against a helpless creature too miserable to be dangerous, didn't stop to think about what she was going to do. She kicked at the soldier's legs and, by chance more than by accurate aim, caught him on the shinbone. He dropped the old man and whirled upon her, howling with pain, hopping on the uninjured leg in such a way that it took him away from her.

"Leave him alone!" Deborah ordered. "Look at him. He's too old to hurt your tyrannical king or your stupid army that's come to put down people who do nothing but seek their rights as human beings—yes, and as Englishmen. Persecutors, that's what you are—

79

all of you! And you! You're nothing but a cowardly, drunken *brute!* Call yourself a soldier? I should think even the British army would be ashamed to own you."

The soldier was, while she was speaking, too concerned with his own pain and too dumfounded to move. But when she was done, he howled again, in anger this time, and started toward her, arms out to grab her. "Another of them," he shouted. "By my faith I've caught two of them."

Too late, Deborah remembered Johnny's warning to go as if she walked on eggs. She knew she must get away and quickly, but her legs seemed paralyzed. Then, thin and receding, she heard the old man's voice, "Run, girl, *run*," and her legs came unstuck and she started to obey, seeing, as she turned, that the soldier's first victim was following his own advice with surprising speed.

The warning gave her the minute she needed to get away, for the soldier, too, had heard and turned to see where the old man was. Torn between going after the man or the girl, the redcoat hesitated before he shouted, "Come back, you!" at Deborah. She ran faster as she heard him start after her. She gave a quick look over her shoulder and saw him stumble over a loose cobblestone and fall. She ran on, twisting and turning, among the many little winding streets until she came at last to the Square, crowded with people. She stopped to get back her lost breath and fix her disheveled hair, feeling safe enough among so many people, before she went slowly home.

Johnny was, for a wonder, there and she told him what had happened, finishing with her long-hoarded apology. "You were right, Johnny. It is best to go about with hidden thoughts." She added to herself, conscious of a glow of pride that she had, at least, told off one of the enemy, "But all the same I shall keep looking and hoping for a chance to help the General. And I'll find a way. You just see if I don't!"

"Did the soldier follow you? Did he know who you were?" Johnny asked, going to the window as if he expected to see the redcoat coming along their street.

"Of course not. I told you he fell and I lost him easily before he could get up. And how could he have known who I was when he had never seen me before?"

Johnny turned and looked at her and started to speak and shrugged his shoulders instead.

"Aren't you glad I got away?" Deborah felt like a deflated pig's bladder, for her tale had certainly fallen flat as the soldier on Johnny's mind.

"Of course, Goose," he said and hugged her. "And I'm gladder still you've seen for yourself that there are dangers to patriots in the city."

She settled, then, more completely into the routine of the house and into her own joy in being part of a proper family. Generally she was aware of nothing but happiness in her new life. But there were things about the household she couldn't understand and they fretted her. There was, first of all, Johnny. There were still many days when he disappeared for hours at a time. She seldom saw him leave even though, after a while, she set herself to watch for his goings. He just wasn't there when she looked for him. Once she asked him where he went.

81

"Oh, here and there," he said, lightly enough, but his face took on a still and watching look as faces do when they are guarding a secret. Deborah decided she'd best not ask again but her curiosity was piqued and she imagined all kinds of dark secrets from which she was excluded, and sometimes she found herself actively resenting Johnny and doubting him.

On one occasion, too, she had come unexpectedly into the room where Lydia was sitting covering button molds. She had moved quietly, not with intent to sneak but because it was her habit, and she had been close beside Lydia before the older woman became aware of her. There had been then a scramble as Lydia swept the button molds out of sight as if they held some sort of guilty secret, and for the first time Deborah had seen her hostess flustered. Neither of them spoke of what had happened but the small mystery stayed in Deborah's mind and came back now and again to puzzle her.

Early in October rumors began to run about the city. Some whispered that General Washington was "up to something"; was, perhaps, preparing to relieve the city of Howe's troops. Others held General Howe was going, any day now, to finish the Continentals once and for all and put an end to this stupid war, sending all the rebel leaders back to England for trial and punishment that would fit the evil nature of their revolt against their lawful king. Nobody knew, in truth, what was happening or about to happen, but all felt a stirring of preparation for something unnamed. The British officers had a waiting look as they stalked about the streets, and the camps of redcoats and Hessians buzzed with excitement.

On the fourth of October the whole town was aware by midmorning that whatever had been about to happen was, at last, happening. Heavy guns could be heard intermittently from the direction of the Germantown Road. All business came to a standstill and many people roamed the streets seeking news.

The Darraghs, restless and worried, stayed indoors all through the morning. No pupils came to William for study. Lydia went about her work with a faraway look and would speak to no one. Johnny roamed from room to room picking things up and setting them down again, obviously not aware of what he was doing.

There's a battle going on, Deborah thought, and they're all sick with worry for Charles. She thought of the bonny face of the young lieutenant in the line of marchers and sought for words to comfort her new friends and could find none. For the first time in this house she felt forlorn, an outsider and a burden upon them all.

Susannah, sitting beside her in the front room, put down the sampler she was reluctantly sewing and whispered, "What's *wrong* with everybody, Deborah? Why is Ma so—so quiet and white? Johnny—Johnny wouldn't even speak to me when I took him my doll to mend." The small face had lost its brightness and was pulled into lines of woe.

Deborah hugged the child and said, "Never mind, Susannah. Johnny'll mend your doll later. Best leave them all alone for a time. Do you come along with me. Get your cloak and we'll go out on the balcony and pretend we're fine ladies in a castle waiting for our knights to come back from the jousting."

Susannah's smile came at once and quickly. She clapped her hands and flew up the wide steps, her woe forgotten.

For an hour Deborah almost lost her own misery as she thought up ways to keep Susannah's mind occupied with games and stories. But the gloom returned when Lydia called them to dinner. Deborah thought the silent meal would never end and she was almost relieved when, toward the end, Susannah broke into a storm of crying that jerked the other Darraghs out of their preoccupation.

"There, there, little one," Lydia said, holding Susannah close against her. "I do believe thee's afraid. But there's nothing to cry about, child. Come along with me. We'll find a sweetmeat I've put by. Johnny, take Deborah and go out and see what can be heard in the town. We've been too close to our worries this day. But mind, be careful."

For once Susannah didn't clamor to go with them, content to stay and be soothed by her mother. Johnny seemed glad to have something to do as he and Deborah left the house. "It's not *knowing*," he said. "It's waiting and waiting and not knowing and not being able to *do* anything."

Deborah wanted to say, "*You* don't know. Suppose you were nothing but a girl and couldn't *ever* do anything but sit and wait," but something told her this was no time to argue with him. She asked instead, "Where is it, Johnny? The battle?"

84

He shook his head. "Wish I knew. Somewhere toward Germantown by the sound of the firing. Somewhere quite near. If Charles—"

"He'll be all *right,* Johnny," she said quickly, yet knowing the words foolish since who could tell which soldiers would be safe and which killed or hurt when a battle was being fought. Her own heart and mind ached to know about Uncle Matt. Was he there, wherever "there" might be? Was he safe? She wondered what a battle was like and tried to make a picture in her mind. But she had nothing to pattern a picture upon. All she could think of was noise and confusion and she felt frightened and lost.

They had been walking aimlessly in the general direction from which the firing had come. People, as aimless as they, were all about them but Johnny made no move to ask questions and she thought he was remembering Lydia's warning to take care lest in some manner he give away his worry for a Continental soldier and so put them all in jeopardy. When they had been gone from the house for perhaps half an hour she was suddenly conscious of the absence of something. She could not place the thing that was missing until a man near her suddenly raised his voice and said, "Hark! It's over. The guns have stopped their firing. If Howe is beaten . . . But he won't be. More likely he's got the dirty rebels on the run."

"Did you hear, Johnny?" she whispered and he began to answer and broke off to listen to a new sound, a dull rumbling sound that came from somewhere ahead of them and off to one side.

"What is it?" Deborah asked.

"Sounds like carts. Come on. Let's find out." He started to run and Deborah ran with him, fighting a new fear she couldn't explain to herself.

They turned into an intersecting street and came at once upon a line of farm carts, the nearest almost upon them. Deborah caught her breath in a sob as she saw the carts full of wounded, most of them in the nondescript clothes, ragged and dirty, that marked them as men of the Continental Army. She could see white faces and bandages, most of them bloody. Some of the men were groaning, others lay still and quiet. Too quiet, she thought.

"Oh, Johnny," she said. "Oh, Johnny," but he didn't hear her. He was standing as close as he could to the path of the carts, watching each pitiful load of misery as it passed slowly, examining the weary, pain-filled faces of the men who lay upon bloody straw in the bottoms of the carts or leaned against the rough wooden sides too exhausted to sit up. He was whispering his brother's name over and over, not knowing he did so. "Charles, Charles, Charles," like a litany.

Deborah's heart reached out to him in pity but she knew she could in no way penetrate the emotion that wrapped him like a dark cloak. Then she too began to examine the carts, searching for Uncle Matt, until the last of the line had passed.

Johnny slowly relaxed his body, which had been taut with fear for his brother, and looked at her. "He wasn't there," he said. "Maybe—maybe all *is* well with him as thee said it would be."

"And, please God, with Uncle Matt," she said softly and he took her hand and gripped it hard and said,

"How *could* we be so forgetful? All this day the Darraghs have had thought for none but Charles. And thee—nobody even remembered Uncle Matt. Forgive us, Deborah, forgive us all for such thoughtlessness. I'm glad, *glad* he wasn't in the carts."

Neither said what was in both their minds, that there was no assurance other men weren't lying wounded or dead somewhere beyond the city. It was enough for now they had not found either of their own in the carts.

"We'd best get back and tell Ma," Johnny said, and they turned toward the Darragh house.

They did not learn the details of the Battle of Germantown until, after dark, Johnny went to answer a soft knocking at the door. The rough sound of the big brass key turning in the lock was loud in the house, reminding them all of the new caution that bade them keep the door, usually fastened only at bedtime, well secured all the day against unwanted intruders. The sound brought William and Lydia from the front room and Deborah from abovestairs where she had been telling Susannah a good-night story. They stood behind Johnny while he said, his hand still upon the key to turn it again quickly if need be, "Who is it?" His voice shook a little as if he were afraid.

"Ebenezer Jordan, Johnny," came the quiet answer. "It's safe to open. I have news."

Johnny jerked the door open and a lanky, grim-faced man with a covered basket on his arm slipped through as Lydia came from the shadows toward him, her face white, her hands outstretched.

"My son?" she asked for greeting.

"Is safe," the newcomer answered. "He has no scratch upon him. I saw him and talked to him not two hours ago."

"Thank God!" Lydia said and covered her face with her hands.

She's going to faint, Deborah thought, and moved toward her, but Lydia stiffened her back and lowered her hands and said, "Thank God" again. She added then, "And thank thee, Ebenezer, for coming quickly to us. Thee is sure *thee* is safe?"

He nodded.

"Hast thee eaten? There's food, such as it is, in the kitchen. We'd best talk there."

As they trailed through the hall to the kitchen, Deborah wondered about Ebenezer Jordan who had come secretly in the dark to relieve the Darraghs' worry. She had not seen him before and there was a look of strain about him as if he were holding himself stiff against the fear of danger, or had been. She thought she would ask Johnny about him but Johnny had again the look of a person guarding a secret and she held her peace. She had a feeling these people were involved in something hidden and the feeling troubled her. Could they be, in truth, spies for the British, in spite of their talk of loyalty to the patriots? At once her mind answered, "Charles." She had herself seen him in the ranks of Washington's army. It was not believable the Darraghs would be helping the enemy that would destroy Charles if it could. She shook her shoulders a little as if by that physical act she could rid herself of the shadow of suspicion that nagged

88

at her mind. But the shadow remained. All she could do was order herself to ignore it and have faith that whatever was going on here it could not be evil.

CHAPTER NINE

The Darraghs listened with long faces as Ebenezer told his story of defeat which might have been worse if George Washington had not had a genius for getting his men out of tight situations. Deborah wondered, seeing their distress, how she could even for a moment have doubted their loyalty to the patriot cause. When Ebenezer had finished his tale, and the food he had been eating the while, he reached for the basket he had placed beside his chair and handed it to Lydia. "They tell it in the byways," he said, "you're feeling the pinch of food hereabouts what with the redcoats having first call on what there is. I managed to keep back some apples and turnips and a bit of bacon. They may help a mite."

Lydia took the basket and for the first time in that long day, her eyes filled with tears as she thanked him. It struck Deborah's mind, then, as if she had felt an actual, physical blow on her skull, she must, in truth, be a burden to the Darraghs, eating food that was so hard to come by. She *should* leave their house at once. She found herself shivering, though the kitchen was warm enough. For if she left them, where could she go? If only she could find Uncle Matt!

Two days later she had her first word of his whereabouts. Johnny came in, late in the afternoon, from one of his mysterious absences. The day was cold and rainy and he went at once to the fireplace in the kitchen and stood before it, his clothes steaming. His mother was, for the moment, out of her beloved kitchen. Deborah, at the spinning wheel, said, "Mercy, Johnny, you look like nothing but a rat drowned in the river."

He grinned at her and said, "I'm neither sugar nor salt. I won't melt," and turned to steam his back before he added, "Besides I've news of Uncle Matt."

"Is he . . . is he . . . ?"

"He's well enough. But he's not at the camp. He's been sent, with others, to reinforce Fort Mifflin on Mud Island."

"Mud Island?"

"In the river. Does thee know the two forts that guard against the coming of the British ships?" He saw the distress and dismay that threatened to set her crying and went on talking to give her time to control the tears. "Seems the General aims to make life hard for the British. If he can keep the supply ships from coming upriver and keep the sniveling, king-loving farmers from bringing in food and fodder from the countryside (that's a large part of what my brother is doing with McLane's Raiders, by the way), he can maybe starve old Howe out. It takes a parcel of stuff to keep an army sharp. Long's the forts—*our* forts—hold, old Howe's brother the admiral can't get by them with his supply ships."

She had found control now and she said steadily, "How did you find out? About Uncle Matt?"

"Oh," he said airily, and there was again that careful blanking of his eyes, "I have my ways."

This time, she thought, I *am* going to ask him further. After all it's *my* uncle and I surely have the right to know where Johnny got his information. But he gave her no time to speak. While she was taking care to choose the right words, he turned from the fire and said, "I must find Ma," and left the room abruptly before she could open her mouth to stop him.

There it was again—that curious, disturbing, unexplainable drawing into himself when she asked him a simple question. What *was* it about these Darraghs? There was surely some mystery in this house but she could find no tag end of a thread that would start her unraveling it. Was Johnny a spy? She wondered, at times, if her imagination, influenced by her own aching and unsatisfied longing to work for the Cause, were conjuring up mysteries that weren't there. But she was sure, most of the time, that she was not imagining the little queernesses that kept recurring.

For now, at any rate, she had been vanquished again by Johnny's withdrawal. She would have to take the information about Uncle Matt on faith. Johnny had, it is true, spoken with assurance and she guessed the source of his information must be sound enough though obviously secret. So now her chance to go to Uncle Matt was lost, at least for a while. She needed no one to tell her she would not be allowed to join him at Fort Mifflin even if she could find a boat to take her there. And the feeling that she should not remain a burden upon the Darraghs kept nagging at her mind. She tried once to tell Lydia she knew she was eating food better conserved for the winter, to offer to leave at once, but Lydia cut short the stumbling effort. "Do not worry thy head, lass. We'll make do," Lydia had said, and Deborah, feeling ashamed at her own relief, accepted the assurance as if she did indeed believe it.

For two weeks after the Battle of Germantown there was no further excitement in the town. But, on the nineteenth of October, General Howe himself, with his large personal staff of officers, appeared without warning and set up his headquarters in a house not a stone's throw from the Darraghs. The next day an officer, very young, very stiff and correct, and very supercilious, came to the door. The uniform he wore, freshly cleaned, its colors shining in the fall sunshine, seemed to mock by its grandness the poor pretensions of the freedom fighters. Johnny was at home and opened the door a crack to insistent knocking. The officer demanded, without courtesy, to see the master of the house.

"My father," Johnny said, deliberately keeping the man standing on the doorstep, "is not at home."

"Your mother, then, boy and quickly." The officer gave Johnny a hard shove that drove his shoulder into the wall with a loud thud and pushed through the door. Deborah, watching from the front room, saw Johnny rubbing his shoulder and fighting to control anger. She wanted to call to him to have a care. She heard him gulp and begin, "My mother . . ."

He got no further. Lydia herself, neat and serene as always, called, "Who is it, my son, comes knocking at our door so loud and rude?"

"An officer of the British Crown, Madam," the intruder

said loudly before Johnny could speak. "And one who is not used to insolence from rebels."

"The lad meant no insolence. Is it always so easy for Crown officers to find offense where none is meant? I had thought courtesy was part of their training. But then thee is, of course, very young."

Deborah wondered if she had imagined Lydia had put a slight extra force upon the Quaker "thee."

Lydia was standing directly before the officer. She had spoken without particular emphasis but with a cold dignity that seemed to shame him. He shifted his feet and, as she went on, actually took off the three-cornered hat. "Besides,"—Lydia looked him straight in the eye—"we are not *rebels* but plain Friends minding our own business. What does thee want?"

"To hand you an order from General Howe, Madam." The officer actually clicked his heels and saluted as he gave Lydia a square of folded paper.

She took and opened it, her fingers steady. Johnny stood beside her. His arms were straight at his sides, his mouth a hard line in a face that had gone from red to white. Deborah could scarcely breathe for the fear that filled her. Had the British found out that the Darraghs were indeed patriots and come to seize them all? She came, too, to stand close to Lydia.

Lydia said, looking straight at the young man, "This is an order requisitioning my house for the use of General Howe's staff." Deborah let out her breath in a long sigh.

"It is, Madam. The General graciously gives you twenty-four hours to evacuate your family."

"And does the General as graciously suggest where I am to take them?"

The officer said nothing.

"We shall see," Lydia said quietly and when the officer still stood in the hallway watching them all with a smug and gloating look as if he enjoyed their discomfiture, she turned to Johnny and said, "Show the—*gentleman* out, my son. His errand is surely finished."

Johnny got the door open and stood beside it until the Britisher, red-faced and almost tripping over his sword, went through it.

"Ma," Johnny said when he was sure the officer was indeed gone, "Ma, what are we going to *do*? We can't go *now*. We can't leave—"

He broke off and looked at Deborah as if he had suddenly remembered her presence. There was in him, she thought, some special urgency which had nothing to do with the problem of finding another place to live. She held her breath waiting for Lydia's answer but Lydia ignored his questions. Instead she said, with a show of that strength Deborah had guessed at, "We'll not be leaving, Johnny. Get my cloak and bonnet, Deborah, if thee please."

Deborah hurried to do as she had been asked and was back in two minutes with Lydia's outdoor clothes. Lydia fastened the gray cloak and tied the matching bonnet firmly and precisely under her chin. She smoothed the dark, knitted gloves over her hands and opened the door and left the house with no further word of explanation.

"Where is she going? What is she going to do?" Deborah asked Johnny.

He shook his head but he was grinning widely and happily. "She didn't say," he answered, "but I'll be bound she'll do *something*. She had the fire in her eye, she did, and I'd hate to be his high-and-mightyness General Howe if he's so bold as to tangle with her. I'd guess her dander's up and thee doesn't know my ma when that happens."

Lydia was back in less than half an hour. She nodded to Johnny and Deborah as she removed the gloves and bonnet and cloak as precisely as she had put them on. "There'll be no more talk of taking our home for *his* officers," she said with satisfaction.

Johnny said, "I told thee, Deborah. Did thee go straight to General Howe, Ma?"

"There was no need. Fortunately our Cousin Barrington was at hand and heard me graciously. He promises we'll hear no more of requisitioning our home, though he spoke of the sometime use of our front room for special assemblies of the British staff should there be such need. He seemed to take it for granted we are loyal to King George and I saw no reason to argue the matter." She smiled and there seemed to Deborah to be a special, secret satisfaction in her eyes. "I thought since I had won the battle, I could well afford to surrender in the matter of a skirmish. I assured our cousin our front room would be at his service when needed."

Johnny hugged her and said, "Good, Ma. Oh, that is very good. Thee's just a wonder," and again Deborah had the feeling the words meant more than they seemed to say.

And that, she thought, would be the end of that. But she was wrong. After supper, when Susannah and Will were both in bed and asleep, Lydia asked Deborah to help a little in the kitchen. Deborah was always eager to do what she could about the house but this request surprised her. Lydia was proud of her kitchen and seldom let anyone else take part in its activities.

As they went about setting the big, cheerful, stone-floored room to rights Lydia told Deborah the time had come to execute a plan she'd had in her mind for some time. "I'd not want the younger children about when the Britishers may be in and out of the house. We've tried to impress upon them the need to watch their tongues, but Susannah, especially, doesn't always think before she speaks. It's best no attention be called to the color of our politics, nor yet to the fact we have a son in the Continental Army. It is not, thee understands, a thing we're not proud of but . . ." She hesitated and, Deborah thought, changed her mind about what she was going to say. "There are reasons we'd not want to spread the word abroad. Besides, food *is* getting scarcer each day, and dearer. It's well enough for us older ones. If we must know the pinch of hunger it will be little enough to suffer for winning our freedom from Royal George's unjust laws. But it's not right for Susannah and Will. They are too young for hardships that can be avoided. And so, I'm going to send them to my cousins, Gideon and Ruth Teele. They have a good farm out along the Germantown Road. The young ones will be well fed through the winter. I'll not go myself, nor William, nor Johnny. It's . . ."—she hesitated again as if she were not sure what she would say, and finished lamely—"*best* we three stay here."

She stopped speaking and turned away from Deborah

and began to poke at her basket of button molds on the table, moving them about idly with one finger as though she were still uncertain about something. Here it is again, Deborah thought, that hint of a mystery. She wondered why Lydia was giving her this long explanation as if she were owed it. She felt somehow embarrassed and wondered if she were expected to say something and cleared her throat a little.

Lydia gave herself a little shake at the sound and turned and went on in a rush. "It would set my mind at rest, lass, if thee would agree to go with the children." She raised her hand as Deborah opened her mouth. "No. Wait. I want to be sure thee knows thee is in no way bound to go. I've come to depend upon thee here as if thee were my own and we will miss thee, Johnny and I. Still, it's the children I'm troubled for. Rather, it's Susannah, for Will will be happy enough with the fields and woods and farm animals for company. But it will go hard with Susannah to leave us. And I thought—if thee wouldn't mind—thee could ease the change for her, for she surely has a fondness for thee. But only if thee *wills* to go. Thee's welcome here always, lass."

Deborah put her arms around Lydia. "Of course, I'll go and gladly if you think it would help Susannah and set your mind at rest," she said and tried to ignore the ache in her heart at the thought of going to strangers just when she had found real happiness and security with the Darraghs.

This, she thought gloomily, would be the very end of her hope to find a way, somehow, to work for freedom. There'd be small chance of anything of that sort on a farm. But what else could she do? She hated even to think where she would be now had the Darraghs not rescued her. The least she could expect of herself was to return their kindness to her in any way she could. That, she reckoned, was her first and most important duty.

Her thinking had taken away her attention from Lydia. Guiltily she brought her mind back. ". . . thee should know," Lydia was saying, "for thy own—own *safety,* perhaps, for it is clear thee would be, if thee could be, the very pattern of a patriot." Lydia paused and shook her head. "Sometimes I wonder if I have done right by thee. Thee would, it may be, have been . . . But never mind now. What's done is done and likely it's— it's best as it is."

Deborah unable to make head or tail of what Lydia was saying interrupted. "I don't understand. What do you mean?"

Lydia shook her head again. "Pay me no heed, Deborah. It's nothing but maundering. Let us get back to my cousins. It's best I warn thee they are—are not of our persuasion nor of our thinking about this war. Gideon's a man not given to change, nor for the matter of that to any form of deep reasoning beyond what's good for the land and the creatures upon it. His farm is a good one and he has been blessed with good crops. He thinks it foolish to—as he puts it—invite disaster by quarreling with King George or those of his representatives sent to the Colonies to govern them. Gideon is not exactly a king-*lover* but he's far from being a king-hater either. He says freedom's nothing but a word and why should he chance his whole life's work for a word. The only freedom he wants, he says, is the freedom to run his farm in his own way and so long as the British leave him to do that he'll not lift hand against them. And he wants no one about him to do anything or say anything that will endanger that position."

Deborah said nothing but "Oh," but her face must have shown her concern at the thought of living with a family no better than Tories, for Lydia went on. "Both my cousins promised, when they begged us to come to them, not to try to change our thinking. Blood, so Ruth says, is thicker than politics and so it is in truth. But it might be best if thee were to guard thy tongue lest it cause an unpleasantness to no purpose."

She stopped and frowned and added, "There's one thing more. When my William went to speak to Ruth of our plans for the children she told of a boy Gideon has lately, for friendship to the boy's uncle and out of pity, given work on the farm. She did not mention his name, only that he was alone in the world and cherishes a passion of hatred against the Continental Congress and all things relating to it. I tell thee this also to prepare thee. It's not likely thee will have much to do with a hired boy. But do thee be careful."

Deborah shivered inside herself wishing she had not so lightly agreed to go to these Teeles. But she *had* agreed and she could not now unsay that promise. She said, as easily as she could from her heavy heart, "I'll be careful."

They left early next day before the city was stirring. The hostler had spread fresh hay in a cart and, when they had bestowed the bundles of clothes and a few toys for Susannah, Will climbed in and rustled the hay delightedly, eager for fresh adventure in a world he loved. At least he's happy, Deborah thought, as Johnny helped her up and lifted a tearful Susannah to sit close to her. He stood at the front of the cart and took the reins and clucked his tongue to start the old horse. Deborah raised her hand to Lydia who stood straight and slim, dry-eyed but somehow forlorn, in the doorway. Poor thing, Deborah thought. The dear only knows when she'll have all her family together again. Then they were off.

It took the ancient mare two hours to cover the distance to the Teeles's farm. They were stopped by a British soldier as they left the city. He questioned Johnny roughly until Johnny showed him the pass issued by General Howe which allowed the Darragh family free exit and entrance as they wished. Even then the soldier, a big, surly man from the north of England whose speech was almost unintelligible to Deborah, was not satisfied. He made them open all the bundles and then get down from the cart while he thrust the bayonet fixed on the end of his musket again and again through the hay. He had, at last, to let them go. When they were a safe distance beyond him Johnny turned and spat toward the place where he stood and began to sing "Yankee Doodle" softly to himself.

CHAPTER TEN

Ruth and Gideon Teele were waiting for them as they came from the road by way of a short lane bordered with maples dressed for autumn in scarlet and gold. Mistress Teele was a middle-aged, comfortable woman with a warm smile and merry eyes. Her husband was courteous enough in his greeting but his face had the look of a man who seldom smiled, and deep creases about his mouth suggested he was a worrier. He had, too, a look of impatience as if he were fretted because he was not about his work.

Mistress Teele fussed over the newcomers, told them breakfast was ready and waiting and seemed distressed when Johnny said he must go straightway to return the horse and cart to the hostler. Deborah's heart ached as, standing beside their bundles of clothes, she bade good-bye, but there was no time to do more than nod when he said, "I'll come back soon as ever I can," for tears were once again running down Susannah's face making wiggly lines in the road dust that had settled there.

"There, there," Mistress Teele said, handing Deborah a clean kerchief to dry Susannah's eyes. "Come and see what there is for breadfast. We'll all feel the better for full stomachs. Leave your bundles where they are, Deborah. Our hired boy'll bestow them in your rooms directly."

Susannah sobbed once or twice as they followed their hostess to the sun-filled kitchen. There a table was set for breakfast, and a scrawny, white-faced kitchen maid named Annie was waiting to serve them. This must be a rich farm, Deborah thought. She had almost forgotten there could be such quantities of food as there were upon the table; such mounds of fresh-baked bread and fresh-churned butter, such a mighty pile of bacon at one end of the table and such a splendor of a roasted fowl at the other. There were, besides, porridge and buckwheat cakes and fried potatoes and fried apples and half a dozen dishes of preserves and jellies and marmalades. She had indeed, never seen such a breakfast, for the Woman had been too mean to set a lavish table and, since the war had come to Philadelphia, only the wealthy hoarders had such plenty. She wished Lydia could be with them.

When they had eaten all they could hold, Mistress Teele led Deborah and Susannah to their room upstairs and said when they were settled they would find her in the kitchen.

Susannah was showing signs of homesickness again and Deborah lost no time in setting her to work putting their clothes in the big walnut chest. When everything was in order she showed Susannah the truckle bed tucked beneath the four-poster which was so big it took up a good part of the room. The child tried to smile at the small bed Deborah said was like a baby chicken huddling under its mother's wings, but her small face was so miserable Deborah sat in the rocking chair by the big window and took her on her lap and told her the story of Jack and the Giant, acting out the parts of the mischievous Jack and making the giant a creature so bumbling and funny Susannah forgot her woe. The story done, Deborah said, "Let's wash our faces and go down now and see if we can help Mistress Teele."

In the kitchen an iron kettle smelling of spices was simmering on a trivet and, as they came back into the kitchen, Annie was just taking a plum cake from the oven built into the brickwork of the fireplace. The cake made Deborah's mouth water but, at the same time, it reminded her the Teeles were British-lovers, for who else could find the currants and spices needed in such trying times as these? She told herself Lydia had said the Teeles would not let their political thinking interfere with their hospitality and hoped she would not, before her stay here was done, forget she was a guest and defend the patriot cause.

Mistress Teele pointed to one corner of the room where a spinning wheel stood with a comb for carding wool beside it. "No one is idle all the day in this household," she explained, smiling at the two girls, "for there is work for many hands upon a good-sized farm like ours. I thought Susannah might help with the carding while you spun the yarn for a time, Deborah."

The morning went quickly. The kitchen was warm and full of good smells. Deborah let her mind rest from fretting and be soothed and comforted by the rhythmic whirring of the wheel as the wool passed smoothly into thread for the myriad needs of the household during the coming winter. She was dreaming of a day when there would be no more war—and she could have her own home and a kitchen like this where she could sit and spin for her own family—when the clatter and clump of the well outside the kitchen door announced that the male members of the family were ready to be fed.

Will came in first, his smiling face ruddy from the crisp autumn day. It was easy to guess he was happy. He would need no coddling in his new surroundings.

Gideon followed the boy closely. Then Deborah had

a shock. A tall, sullen-looking boy pushed awkwardly through the door and, without looking at any of them, plumped himself down at the table. "This is our new hired boy, Rob Bates," Mistress Teele said, but the words came to Deborah with a faraway sound, for she knew this untidy great hulk of a boy.

Her mind spun and wheeled. It couldn't very well be worse. So *this* was that hired boy Lydia had spoken of who hated rebels with a violence beyond reason. Her whole body shook and quivered with the fear she had been able to ignore only because there had been at the Darraghs nothing to stir it where it slept hidden in her mind. This Rob Bates was the leader of the gang that had tormented Johnny on the day of the march-by of General Washington's army. And she was afraid of him. Dear heaven, how she was afraid! She sat very still at her wheel, feeling her fear prickling the fine hairs on the back of her neck, wondering what he would do when he looked up and recognized her.

"Come, Deborah," Mistress Teele said and, after a sharp look at her, added, "Are you all right, child? You're as white as a new-washed lamb."

Deborah forced her mind away from fear. "I—it's nothing, Mistress," she said. "I think I was just dizzy for a minute. From watching the wheel. I am, truly, all right now."

She got up from the stool beside the wheel and went slowly to her place at table, furious that her lagging might have drawn Rob's attention to her. She was sure he would not be one to forget a grudge, and surely he would consider her action in saving Johnny as cause for a grudge. Likely she would have to face his anger some time. But she wanted a little while to get used to the idea of his being here before she must do so. While their heads were all bowed for the blessing before the meal she swiveled her eyes at him, expecting to find him glaring at her. But he gave no sign he had noticed anything out of the ordinary. Throughout the meal he kept his disagreeable look upon his plate, stacked with huge quantities of food, and ate steadily. Only when the meal was done and Gideon had said, "Time to work," did he give her one quick, piercing, malevolent look as he left the house. She knew then he had recognized her and would surely bring trouble to her—and perhaps to Johnny.

Johnny! He must be warned. He couldn't have known about Rob's presence here, for if he had he would surely have cautioned her about it. Mistress Teele was speaking about Rob now to Annie, and Deborah turned her mind to listen.

". . . that Rob! I just can't get him to take any care for common neatness in his dress and person. He plain likes to be dirty, I think. I wish to goodness Gideon had never taken him on, even if he was left alone when *they* sent his uncle to Virginia, drat the brutes! Nothing would do but Gideon must give the—the oaf a place to live and work to do. He's ever soft for lone, lorn things, is my Gideon. But there'll be trouble with Rob Bates, mark you what I say."

"Tch, tch!" Annie, always sparing with words, clucked soothingly and Mistress Teele, feeling the better, Deborah thought, for having had her say, sighed and went back to her work.

Deborah decided the only thing she could do was try

to stay out of Rob's way. He was, at least for the moment, not likely to trouble her since Gideon had said they would work the north field until dark and would, therefore, be later than usual coming in for their supper. Maybe by tomorrow she could think of some plan to avoid him.

The next morning Mistress Teele asked Deborah to take Susannah to the apple orchard to pick up what culls were left on the ground. "They aren't fit for us to eat," she said, "but as the saying goes, 'Waste not, want not,' and the pigs will not care if they're speckled."

Deborah didn't want to leave the house. Gideon and Rob and Will had already gone to the fields when Mistress Teele had called her and Susannah to their breakfast and she didn't know where Rob Bates would be today. The night had brought no end to worrying about him and she was still not ready to meet him. But she could hardly refuse the request and so she got her shawl and another for Susannah and went along the path Annie pointed out.

The orchard was not far from the house and Deborah was relieved clear down to her boots when she could see nothing among the trees but a flock of sheep that promptly took to their heels, the silly creatures, when she and Susannah appeared.

Susannah was fretful and lagging as they began to fill a sack from a pile under one of the trees. She was not accustomed to this kind of work and it was, indeed, not easy. Deborah's back began to ache with the constant bending and stretching before the sack was a quarter full. Nor were the dropped apples easy to find, for the sheep had trampled many in the long grass, birds had pecked at some until little more than a shell was left, and bees buzzed angrily about others whenever the girls came near. By the time they had filled the sack they had searched under all the trees, and Susannah was whimpering a little with fatigue and wishing she could go home. Deborah stood the sack, heavy now, against a tree and sat on the grass beneath it pulling Susannah down beside her. "Just let me rest a little, Suzy," she said. "I'll tell you a story while my back unkinks itself. By then it'll likely be time for dinner."

Susannah huddled close to her and she put her arm around the drooping shoulders and began an ancient tale about an old woman and a disobedient child who stole a bag of money and ran away with it. The tale had in it a recurring jingle that went

> Seen a little gal come by here
> With a jig and a jag and a long feather bag
> And all the money I ever had since I was
> a knee high!

Deborah chanted the refrain, as Uncle Matt had taught her to do, in a high thin wail of a voice, and after the first time Susannah joined in. By the end of the story the child had forgotten her tiredness and was almost doubled in two with delighted laughter at the witch faces Deborah had made. Deborah laughed with her, glad she could drive away gloom with stories and her gift for mimicry. She was still laughing as she got up and pulled Susannah to her feet, ready to start back to the house.

"*Thee* has nothing to laugh about, r-r-rebel!"

The words came from behind them and Deborah whirled about, guessing who she would find but hoping she would be wrong. She was not wrong. Rob Bates stood glaring at her with such anger and dislike she felt as if he had hit her. He had come so quietly through the long grass between the trees she hadn't heard him and surprise gave an added edge to the fear that had been half hidden in her mind. Susannah made a little frightened sound and hid herself behind Deborah's wide skirts.

"What do you want?" Deborah asked. She was surprised to find her voice steady because her hands were shaking. She held them straight at her sides, balling them into fists to still them.

"To call thee to dinner." He managed to make the simple sentence sound as sharp as a threat and with his next breath put the threat into words. "*And* to tell thee I well remember thee and thy interfering ways. We are loyal subjects of our rightful king here and we'll not abide rebellion, nor yet interference with teaching rebels a lesson they'll not soon forget."

He stopped and waited for some comment, his little, cruel eyes never leaving her face. When she gave him no answer he went on, "*Well!* What does thee say? I'll thank thee to show proper respect, my lady."

Suddenly Deborah was so angry at his presumption she forgot the fear she'd been at such pains to hide from him. What right had he, who was only a hired boy taken on for charity, to lecture her, to *threaten* her? She was a guest in this house. What she thought of the war was no business of his. If the Teeles were satisfied he had no cause to interfere. She stood straight and thought of Uncle Matt offering his life for the cause of liberty. She returned his look steadily and said, "I am no *rebel*. Nor are any of us rebels who seek liberty and justice and freedom from a cruel king and his unjust laws. And I will—"

"Liberty! Justice! Freedom!" He threw the words back at her as if he wished they were stones to hurt her. "Words. Nothing but words."

"They are *not* just words," she said. "They are—they are the spirit of this country. It's not *right* for one man far, far away in London town to grow rich and fat on the labor of thousands of his subjects. Subjects! Aren't we as human as he is? Haven't we got the right to live our own lives and think our own thoughts without his telling us how? Haven't we the right to work for ourselves without paying out almost every bit we can earn in his stupid old taxes we have no say about? Yes, I know all about your old uncle, how he's been sent away because he's likely a danger to the Congress and its plans. But if he'd only promised not to make trouble he'd be here now, safe and sound. You just wait and see, Rob Bates. We'll run the redcoats out of the *United States* before we're done. You just wait!"

"United States," he said and spat on the ground beside him. "I'll wait. Oh yes, I'll wait. And I'll *watch*. And if I catch thee so much as whispering one more word of sympathy for the rebels, *thee'll* be the one to see. For I'll find a way to make thee pay for thy treachery to the king."

He started to turn away and she thought he had finished and wished she could find a good retort. But he turned back again and added with such menace she could almost have thought he was the devil himself, "And if I see that Johnny Darragh here I'll finish what I started that other day." Then he disappeared through the trees as silently as he had come, leaving her to wrestle with the heavy sack of culls.

She felt too numb to think about his threats as she got hold of the neck of the sack ready to drag it back to the barn. Susannah's eyes were huge as she tagged along. "What's the *matter* with that boy, Deborah?" the child asked. "He frightened me. He's *mean.*"

"Never you mind, Suzy," Deborah smiled at her and wished she could believe her own words. "He's nothing but a big bully. He'll not harm you. Help me pull now, and we'll come the sooner to our dinners. I'll warrant you're hungry as—as a big black bear in the hills when he's just waking up from his winter's sleep."

CHAPTER ELEVEN

Deborah was quiet during dinner. She wasn't hungry in spite of her morning's work and did no more than pick at the food until the meal was over. She wanted to get away from all of them, even Susannah; get off by herself and think about Rob Bates and his threats. Maybe he *was* just a bully as she had told Susannah. She tried to reassure herself that there was really nothing he *could* do to her, not if she were careful never to be alone with him. But still a thread of fear nagged at her mind. *Could* she be sure she'd never meet him when no one else was nearby?

When, the meal over, Mistress Teele asked Susannah if she'd like to go and look for eggs, Deborah saw her chance to do her thinking and got her shawl and started to walk down the lane to the main road. But even alone she found her mind wouldn't work clearly. The brilliance of the autumn colors around her; the sight of a flight of wild geese, late flying in their wedge-shaped formation toward the warmth of southern lands; the crisp feel of the pleasant October day distracted her. She came to the empty road and stood looking toward the town with her thoughts still roiling like a stream in spring flood. She wished she were back in the friendly security of the Darragh home. She wished she could see Uncle Matt, just for a minute; could hear his dear, familiar voice telling her not to be a ninny. She wished at least she could talk to Johnny.

As if her wishing had been a fairy spell, she saw him. He had, she guessed, come by the short way over the wood path. He appeared at the edge of a copse that bordered the road and jumped the ditch and saw her and waved his hand. When he came up to her she said, "Oh, Johnny!" and he knew instantly she was troubled and asked, "What is it Deborah? What's the matter?"

She told him in a rush about Rob Bates and saw her fears reflected in his face. Strangely enough his worry made her feel at once relieved that she was not being stupidly frightened and, at the same time, more deeply concerned for the predicament she was in.

"Let's go along to the house as we talk," he said. "I promised Ma I'd see with my own eyes that Susannah is well and not too unhappy."

He took her arm as they walked and the feel of his

hand brought her comfort and reassurance in spite of his words. "I don't like it, Deborah, and that's the truth. This Rob—he's a case for pity and I feel it for him in truth. But he's—he's half mad, I think, and dangerous."

"What makes him so—so wild, then, sometimes? Other whiles he's biddable enough, or seems so, though he's always surly."

"Indeed it's hard to know, Deborah. I've heard it said his mother, who was ever a sad, lorn creature, was found drowned in the farm pond when Rob was no more than four years old. Some say she did away with herself in a fit of despondency. His father was always a —a sullen soul and when the lady died he drew ever more into himself and would speak to no one until, finally, he disappeared and no one's heard of him since."

"And left the little lad alone?"

Johnny nodded. "But not for long. Rob's uncle, his mother's oldest brother and a bachelor, took Rob and raised him as his own son. He was an upright man, that uncle, and stern beyond the common, but Rob loved him well. Then the uncle was sent away to Virginia, suspected of giving help to the British, and Rob changed from a peaceable-enough soul to—to what he is now. It's as if he lost his wits—or some part of them—with grieving and brooding over what he calls injustice. And so he's dangerous, as any part-wit can be. If Ma weren't so—so worried," (Deborah thought he'd started to say something else and changed his mind just in time to preserve his secret, whatever it was) "I'd tell her about all this and ask her to bring thee back. But—"

She broke in. "Don't you *dare* add to your mother's

worries, Johnny Darragh. I promised, of my own will, I'd look after Susannah and I intend to do it."

"Then be careful when Rob's at hand. Very careful. Is he often in the house?" His hand on her arm clutched spasmodically as if to emphasize his warning and he scowled at her as if he were angry. "Maybe I should talk to Aunt Ruth."

She shook her head impatiently. He sounded as if she were indeed a ninny. His concern served to lessen hers and she decided he was making too much of the danger. She said, "Give over Rob. I'll not have you making a fuss on my account, nor interfering between your Uncle Gideon and his good works. Besides that, Rob only comes into the house for meals. He's gone before I even get up. It's not likely he'll do me harm in the kitchen with Mistress Teele and the master looking on. After all, I'm a girl and I doubt he'll *beat* me. It's you I'm mostly worried for."

"I'm not afeared of him. But thee be careful. If he is truly near to madness he might forget thee's a girl, and he's stronger than most. Promise thee'll be *extra* careful the whole time."

"I promise," she said, and was a little relieved to have their gloomy talk ended by Susannah. She came hurtling around the house and threw her arms about Johnny, telling him in a rush about the baby chicks she'd found in the barn.

They had been at the Teele farm for a month before Rob Bates made any more threats. Deborah had, to a large extent, lost her fear of him, for she saw him, as she had predicted, only at meals. Though he scowled he never spoke to her. Indeed he didn't speak at all unless it were necessary. His untidy, grumpy presence did nothing to enliven their mealtimes but Mistress Teele and her husband managed to ignore him and Deborah could forget him when he was not in the house. She wondered what he did when he went to the boxlike cubicle off the stillroom where he slept. Sulked, most likely.

Johnny was responsible for Rob's next outburst. Johnny came once or twice a week to the house to bring them news of the Darraghs and Philadelphia and to take back assurances to Lydia that all was well with them. The war, at least that part of it that centered on Philadelphia, seemed for the most part to have come to a standstill except for occasional bursts of activity now and then. McLane's Raiders, Johnny said, were everywhere, seeking news of British plans, preventing the king-lovers who lived on farms from bringing food to the hungry city. Fort Mifflin fell in spite of a heroic defense and was burned on November 16 by the retreating garrison, but, Johnny reassured her—and again turned aside her questions as to how he knew—Uncle Matt was safe and attached to Washington's headquarters which the General was going to move from the Skippack Road to Whitemarsh farther away from the city and, hopefully, safer from British attack. Eleven thousand patriots had left the city and many of their shops and houses had been seized by Tories from the south who had come to Philadelphia where they would be unmolested if not actually welcomed.

Mistress Teele was always glad to see Johnny and he was careful to wait to give his news until she was out of the room where he talked to Deborah and Susannah. "No sense riling her," he said, "and the dear knows I can't pretend to like the redcoats or what they're doing. Best leave the war alone when she's nearby."

He had been to the farm half a dozen times before he came face to face with Rob Bates. Then, on a day that was cold and dreary with the first wet snow of the year sifting down in big, soft, lazy flakes from a dull gray sky, Rob discovered him. Johnny was standing before the kitchen hearth warming his hands at the big logs that gave off a summer fragrance with their burning. Mistress Teele had greeted him and taken Annie upstairs to get out the extra blankets from the lavender-scented storage chests where they had been packed away for the summer. Susannah was playing with her doll in a corner of the room and Johnny was telling Deborah of a disaster to the American ships which had attempted to sneak past the British and sail above Philadelphia during the night of the twenty-first of November. The sound of explosions had wakened the city in the early morning and Johnny had gotten out of his bed and dressed hurriedly and walked down to the wharf. "My heart fair turned over with sickness at the sight, Deborah. All our ships, coming upriver with the flood tide, in a fury of fire. We heard afterwards their crews had set them ablaze and abandoned them when it was plain they were discovered and would be taken by the British. Four of them blew up entirely. And, oh, it was a sad sight and one I'm not like to be forgetting do I live to be an hundred."

Deborah was saying, "Poor, poor General Washington," when Rob Bates banged the door open and stomped in, not bothering to wipe the snow from his boots, and heard her. "I told thee," he shouted at her, "I told thee I'd have no mooning over the rebels or conniving with a rebel-lover who, like as not, is spying out news for his Continental soldier brother! What is thee doing here, renegade Friend, persecutor of innocent men?"

White-faced, Johnny started to speak and, when his voice came out in a high, thin squeak he stopped and cleared his throat and began again, answering the question as if it had been an ordinary one and no challenge. "I was on my way to Frankford Mill for flour and stopped to see my sister."

The simple explanation seemed to distract Rob for a moment. He shook his head from side to side like a troubled child and the red drained away from his face. Deborah was beginning to think that by some magic Johnny had satisfied him when he gave his head a final, violent shake and shouted, "And if thee do be going to mill where's thy sack? Tell me that, rebel and traitor."

Deborah thought he would never answer the question and waited, holding her breath, wondering why indeed he had no sack and why he had claimed to be going to the mill in the first place, while the rest of her willed him to speak up.

"*Answer* me, then, if thee can!" Rob Bates was still shouting, and Johnny cleared his throat again and said in a rush, "I left the sack at the mill, for the miller was away and the mill locked. His good wife told me to go and come again later for the full sack."

"A likely tale!" Rob said. "I know what thee is about,

Johnny Darragh. Thee's up to some mischief against the king. And it's me, Rob Bates, who'll stop thee."

Deborah thought Johnny looked as if he had been hit by a bullet from a redcoat's musket. She saw Rob start toward him, big, hamlike hands reaching. She knew she must do something and was too held by fright to think what she could do. She tried to scream out for Mistress Teele and could make no sound.

They had all forgotten Susannah, had not noticed she had dropped her doll and sidled out of the kitchen when Rob first began to shout at Johnny. Now, before the dreadful hands could seize Johnny, she came back tugging at Mistress Teele's skirts.

"Rob Bates!" Ruth Teele's voice cracked in the tense room. The sound stopped Rob's rush toward Johnny and she went on, "What *is* this? Frightening the child with your shouting, and threatening Johnny and Deborah. What do you think you're doing here in my kitchen?"

"He's—he's—" Rob couldn't seem to get the words out of his writhing mouth.

Mistress Teele waited.

"He's—a *rebel!*"

"Is that any business of yours? You'll be pleased to remember Johnny Darragh is my cousin and a guest in my house and you will treat him accordingly."

"But, Mistress, thee doesn't understand. . . ."

"I understand you're beside yourself. Do you not try my patience too far, Rob Bates, or you'll find yourself homeless again. Now get back to your duties outside. At *once.*"

"But, Mistress Teele—"

She would not listen to him. "I said *go.* I mean it.

Or do you want me to call the master and have him force you? And do you listen to me well. No politics and no war will come between me and my kin *or* their friends. You are here by my sufferance, for my husband will send you away if I insist upon it. Remember that when next you try to pit your will against mine."

Rob tried to stare her down but could not. He had to circle Johnny as he shambled toward the door. Passing him he muttered, "I know a good deep pond. Next time I won't be—"

"Rob!"

He gave Johnny and Deborah one last, hating look and went out, banging the door so hard behind him the heavy spit shook in the fireplace.

Johnny wiped his hand across his forehead and said, "Whew!" Mistress Teele apologized for the hired boy's behavior. "I don't know what gets into him," she said. "He used to be a good, steady lad but when *they* took his uncle—I'm sorry, Johnny, but I cannot approve of *that*—something happened to him. Sometimes I think he's plain bewitched. But don't fear, Johnny. I'll talk to Gideon and he'll see nothing like this will happen again."

"No, Cousin Ruth," Johnny said, "likely not. Do thee not fret on my account."

But later, when Deborah and Susannah, well bundled up, were walking with him down the lane to the road, he said, "Cousin Ruth is right. What happened today will *not* happen again. For I'll not let it. I'll not come back to the house."

"But, Johnny," Deborah began to argue, feeling lost at the thought she would not see him again, "I doubt he'll be a danger to you now Mistress Teele has promised to tell the master."

"Be quiet, Deborah!" Johnny said, speaking roughly to her for the first time since she had known him. "There be things thee doesn't know of. I'll not risk another tangle with Rob Bates—for reasons of my own—and that's the end of it."

She felt unjustly rebuked and hurt and took her hand from the crook of his arm and drew a little away from him. For a minute they walked along with silence separating them as surely as if it had been a stone fence set between them, while Susannah skipped ahead unconscious of the strain. Then Johnny said, quietly, matter-of-factly, as if he had never spoken to her in anger, "I can't know just when I'll be passing, Deborah. But I'll be coming this way again and again, often enough each week. And I'll manage to come at just about the same time—say an hour after dinner's done. Best thee comes each day with Susannah to the road. That way I'll be sure to see thee whenever—whenever some errand for Ma brings me by."

She looked at him wonderingly. How could he rebuke her so harshly one minute and, without apology or explanation, tell her what to do the next? I'll not do it, she thought. I'll not have him ordering me about like a slave girl. But she knew she would do as he asked, for she would rather forget her own hurt pride than go through all the dreary days without his sometime companionship.

"All right," she said, not very graciously.

They had come to the road. He ignored her grudging tone and swung Susannah up for a hug. "Every day," he said, "an hour after dinner's done," and went down the road toward the town singing his favorite, "Yankee Doodle."

A full week passed before Deborah saw him again. The snow had been the harbinger of the first hard cold spell of the winter and Susannah had come down with the quinsy and was still abed but recovering. Deborah had found it hard to get to the road but she had managed and been the more disappointed when Johnny was absent. Now, seeing Susannah happy with her doll and Mistress Teele sewing in the rocking chair by the window, Deborah hurried down the lane, not expecting Johnny yet not daring to miss her daily appointment with him lest he come and find her absent. She walked quickly, pulling her cloak close about her against the biting wind that sang in the bare, black trees. She came to a bend in the lane from which she could glimpse the place where it joined the road and saw the junction empty. She felt forlorn and forsaken and almost hated Johnny because he had betrayed his promise to come and left her lonely with no one to companion her throughout the long week. She thought she would turn back to the house, not bother to wait upon the chance of his late coming. But a corner of her mind still held to the hope she would see him this day and she went on.

She stood, hunched and unhappy, looking down the empty road until a low moaning prickled her scalp. She could not tell whether the sound was human or animal but it was, without doubt, a sound of pain. She squinted her eyes against the brilliant afternoon sun and could still see nothing and began to move cautiously toward the sound.

Then she saw Johnny. He was sitting on the ground, his back against the bole of a tree, one foot cradled in his hands. She ran toward him, calling his name and he stopped moaning and tried to smile reassurance at her.

She squatted on her heels beside him saying his name over and over, feeling helpless at the sight of the pain lines on his face.

"Thank heaven thee has come, Deborah," he said. "I was afeared thee'd given me up."

"What is it, Johnny? What's happened to you?"

"It's my ankle." He made a face so wry it almost brought a laugh from her in spite of her anxiety for him. "The more fool me," he went on. "I was so busy thinking about—about *things*," (even now, she thought, there's that mystery) "I forgot to mind my way and stepped spang into a rabbit hole yonder"—he pointed across the road toward the wood path—"and fell a-sprawling on my face. I managed to get across the road, but I had to crawl like a silly worm because my ankle got caught under me when I fell and now it won't hold me up."

She was on her feet, working to unfasten her cloak for she saw his whole body shaking with the cold. "I'll go to the house for help," she said. "Here,"—the stubborn button had at last come unfastened—"you'd best take my cloak. I'll run the way back and—"

He stopped her. "No, Deborah," he said and looked at her as if he would see inside her very heart, his eyes showing the uncertainty in his mind.

"But, Johnny, you can't—"

"Hear me, Deborah." He pulled himself higher against the tree and his eyes lost the uncertain look as if he had come to a decision he would hold to no matter what the consequences. "And while thee listens, gather the dead leaves and cover me. Nothing like leaves to keep out the cold. There's a thing I must tell thee though none should know of it. But there's no help for it now. Will thee give me thy solemn promise thee'll never tell what thee's going to hear? Never unless I give thee leave?"

She put her hand over her heart and said, "I promise, Johnny. You know I'll promise and I'll keep my word."

"I believe thee," he said. "Now hear me. And get about gathering those leaves for I'm near to loosing my teeth with their chattering." He smiled at her then and she felt better as she found a fallen branch and used it to rake together armloads of leaves while he talked.

CHAPTER TWELVE

"Thee has wondered, Deborah," Johnny began while she piled leaves over him and saw his shivering lessen a little as warmth began to creep over his body, "if we had a secret, Ma and I, for I've seen thee wondering and wanted to tell thee and dared not. Ma almost told thee once, the day the redcoat came to our house, but she thought it safest not to. Safest for us and safest for thee and safest, likely, for General Washington's plans. But now it's me must decide and there's nothing to do but risk it, for Charles must get the message within the hour or he'll be gone."

"The message?"

"Now listen and ask no questions," he said. "General Washington needs to know all he can about the British in Philadelphia. Even little things like the way the officers spend their time could mean a big difference to him if he thinks he can drive the British away from the city. He's got a whole—a whole *net* of spies in and around the city with ways of getting information to him so they'll not be caught. And we're part of it—Ma and Pa and me."

"*You,* Johnny?" She ignored his order not to ask questions in her excitement.

"Yes, me." He had forgotten about his ankle as he talked and had shifted his position and now he cried out sharply with the pain. She started toward him but he twisted his face into the semblance of a grin and said again, "Yes, me. When one of us hears something, even some very small thing about the British and what they're doing, Pa writes a message in shorthand he learned while he was still a boy in Ireland. Ma puts the message in a button mold and covers it over with cloth and sews it on my coat and I take it to the Rising Sun Tavern to Charles. Then Captain McLane can send it straight on to the General. Captain McLane is chief of all the spies just now."

He had been tugging at his coat and, with a little snap, a thread broke and he had a button in his hand. He held it out to her and she looked at it stupidly, wondering why he was offering it to her and when he would tell her what he wanted her to do. Her mind

124

was filled with surprise at his story and with admiration for him and his family and envy that he could have so active a part in helping the fight for liberty while she, being nothing but a girl, must stand idly by.

"Here," he said, a little impatiently, "take it."

She did as he told her and asked, "What shall I do with it?"

"Haven't you been *listening*, Deborah? Take it to Charles at the Rising Sun Tavern as I said."

"Me?" He was asking her to take his place; asking her, a useless girl, to act as courier for General Washington's spymaster. She must have heard all this in her wishful mind. He couldn't be trusting her *that* far! She said again, "Me?"

"Who else? Unless thee is afraid. And mind thee," he added quickly, "I shouldn't blame thee if thee were for there *is* some danger. Not much, but a little. And if thee'd rather not, I'll—I'll have to think of another way."

"Of *course* I'm not afraid." She almost shouted the words, thinking he must be a little crazy with pain to think she would not rush to do his bidding in this.

"Then thee'd best be going. Thee'll not miss the Rising Sun for it sits close by the Germantown Road. It's not above three miles from here. Thee should be there in less than an hour if no one stops thee. There'll be sentries about the inn. Ask one of them for Lieutenant Darragh and say his mother sent thee with a message for him. Will they miss thee at the house? Thee'll likely be away overlong."

"I'll say I walked in the woods over the road and lost my way and was a time finding it again. But, Johnny,

125

what of you? If you just lie here you'll likely freeze or take the quinsy."

He made an impatient gesture. "Hurry, Deborah. Don't stand there dithering. Thee'll likely meet Ebenezer Jordan on the road. He's one of us and safe. Tell him where to find me. But don't tell even him the errand. Charles says it's best one spy doesn't know what the others are doing. It's safer so for everybody. If Ebenezer asks thee where thee is going, say—say Mistress Teele sent thee to the miller at Frankford. And tell Charles not to worry. Ma'll fix this pesky ankle. Tell him I'll surely come myself next time I've a loose button."

She hesitated for one more minute. What he had said explained many things that had puzzled her since she had come to the Darraghs. But new questions she'd been too dazed to ask were crowding her mind, and she wanted to put them all in a rush. Johnny said again, "Hurry!" and, at last, his urgency infected her and she left him, almost running down the road toward Germantown.

Half a mile further on she met Ebenezer Jordan as Johnny had promised, and saw with relief he was driving a tumbledown cart. A jumble of baskets half filled with spotted apples and undersized turnips and potatoes covered the cart bottom but there would be room for Johnny too. The spavined mare plodding between the shafts was willing enough to stop at Ebenezer's "Whoa" and she told him about Johnny. He looked at her with curiosity, sensing perhaps her haste and tension and wondering about it, but he asked no questions and she was glad, for a lie, even a lie in a good cause, came hard to her.

She hurried on, fearful each moment she would meet a British soldier or a Hessian and be stopped. She had slipped the button inside her heavy knitted glove and she kept her hand closed in a fist and hidden inside her cloak. What would she do with the button if she were stopped? She would, she reckoned, have to depend upon some inspiration of the moment to account for it. She wished she knew of a way through the woods where she would be a little sheltered by the trees; a way where she would feel less exposed to curious passersby, but she was too unfamiliar with the countryside to risk trying to find such a safer path.

She almost cried out with relief when she saw just ahead of her the low, friendly shape of a house and recognized the symbol of the rising sun upon the painted sign that swung from a post beside it. She walked confidently to the door and was stopped by a man in a ragged hunting shirt who threw his long rifle across the door to bar her way.

"What's your name and business?" he asked harshly in a twanging voice that told her he came from some other part of the country.

"D-d-deborah S-s-stone," she stammered, more frightened by his stern suspicious face than she had been by her lonely walk. "I—I have a m-m-message for Lieutenant Charles D-d-darragh from his mother."

"I've got no orders from the lieutenant to let any" —he looked her up and down—"little girl in to him. Let's see your pass from the General."

She was feeling more and more panicky and her

voice rose as she said, "I've got no pass from the General. But I must see Lieutenant Darragh. I *must*, I tell you. It's important. Please let me in, or anyway go and tell him I'm here."

"*Nobody* goes inside without I know them or without I'm expecting them or without they've got a pass. And if you think I'm a-going to pester the lieutenant for a chit of a girl you're just wrong. Now be off with you and leave me to my sentry go." He made a shooing motion with the rifle and the bayonet on its end caught the sun and shone menacingly.

"Please," Deborah said, tears of anger and frustration and uncertainty spilling over her eyelids. "Please. Please. *Please.*"

"Now see here, you," the sentry began, and was interrupted by a voice from the shadows behind the opened door of the inn. "What's all the noise, Jenkins? We can't hear ourselves think in here."

Jenkins said over his shoulder, not taking his eyes from Deborah, "Some young chit as *says* she's got a message for you, Lieutenant—" He got no further. Deborah pressed as close to the door as the rifle would permit and called out, "Please, Lieutenant Darragh. Johnny sent me. He's hurt his ankle and couldn't come himself."

"What's thy name?" The lieutenant still didn't come where she could see him and she thought he's afraid I may be a spy for *them* and doesn't want me to be able to recognize him.

"Deborah Stone," she said and prayed Johnny had mentioned her and the lieutenant would remember.

"Pass the young lady in, Jenkins."

Jenkins stepped to one side grounding the rifle as he did so. "If you say it, Lieutenant. But I don't know as I like it much."

"I'll be responsible, Jenkins," Charles Darragh said, and stepped out of the shadows to offer Deborah his arm. She took it as if she had been a grand lady going to a ball and as she passed the sentry she turned and stuck out her tongue at him, finding relief in the childish gesture from the stored tensions of the last hour.

She had a dim impression of other men in the big, cold hall, standing in small groups or scurrying about. But she had no time to look about her. Charles Darragh opened a door on the right and stood aside for her to go before him into an empty room where a fire burned cheerfully and a long table of bare boards scrupulously clean was set for a meal.

"Now," he said when he had shut the door, "what is all this about?" He was polite enough but there was more than a little sternness in his face and more than a little suspicion.

She took off her glove and held out the button, surprised to see on her palm an angry red mark where she had clutched it too hard, and to feel an ache that seemed to go right through to the back of her hand. At the sight of the small cloth-covered thing she saw his face relax and the sternness and suspicion go out of it.

"Is Johnny ill?" he asked then in a voice that showed such loving concern for his younger brother that she hurried to reassure him, telling him the story of Johnny's accident and giving him the message that he was not to worry for this was but a small thing and temporary.

He thanked her then, turning the button over and

over upon his own palm, and questioned her closely about who she had met upon the road. She told him only Ebenezer Jordan who had promised to get Johnny home and asked no questions about her mission and Charles seemed immensely relieved.

"How does thee plan to get back?" he asked.

"Walk," she said, wondering how else.

"Best not. No need to rouse Cousin Ruth's curiosity more than need be by coming later than you must. Best she have as little cause as possible to wonder. Do thee wait here but a moment. I'll get my cloak and my horse. He's tired but thee is not such a weight he can't carry double for a mile or two."

He was back almost as quickly as he'd promised. She noticed he no longer had the button. "It's already on its way to the General," he told her with a smile. "Come now."

He led her through a series of rooms to a yard where a black horse stood, ready saddled, patiently waiting. He mounted and leaned down and lifted her easily to the crupper and told her to hang on to him. Then he walked the horse out of the yard into a thick wood and along paths that were obviously as familiar to him as his own hand until they were in sight of the Teele farm.

"Two minutes will see thee home, Deborah Stone," he said, breaking the silence as he set her down. "My thanks and the General's for thy work this day. Thee has struck a blow for liberty this day, girl. Would all hereabouts were as willing to do as much."

He drew himself straight in the saddle and gave her a formal salute and wheeled the horse smartly and rode away while she stood tongue-tied at his praise. When he was out of sight she turned toward the house feeling so full of pride and happiness she thought her heart would burst with it.

But a few minutes later her pleasure gave way to uneasiness. She came quietly into the house by the kitchen door and saw Susannah wrapped in a blanket, clutching her doll and sitting in one of the armchairs by the table, her small face screwed into a frown of worry. Mistress Teele was beside her, speaking softly. "Nothing *can* happen to our Deborah, child. Not here in our peaceful countryside. She likely walked longer than she intended for she's had little chance to exercise her legs these past days for caring for you. She'll be along directly, you mark my words."

"I'm here now, Mistress Teele," Deborah said quietly and jumped when an angry voice behind her asked, "What has thee been up to now, Mistress?"

Mistress Teele said, "Rob!" sharply and went on quietly enough, though her voice carried a note of reproof, "Where *have* you been, Deborah? Indeed we have all been upon the point of worrying."

Rob dumped the armload of wood he was carrying noisily on the hearth and watched her sullenly. Annie sniffled as she lifted one of the logs and threw it on the fire. Mistress Teele and Susannah kept their eyes on Deborah silently, and she felt alone among them.

She was, suddenly, bone-tired and limp with reaction to the excitement of the day. She had rehearsed her answer to this expected question half a dozen times on the ride back from the Rising Sun until she had been prepared, she had thought, to give it glibly, but now

131

the well-learned words deserted her and she stammered, "I—I thought. . . ."

She paused to control the shaky feeling deep inside her that threatened to set her teeth chattering and thought of Johnny and knew she must not endanger his secret. The thought steadied her and she went on more calmly. "I thought to explore a little beyond the farm and I saw something, some strange animal tracks and started to follow them and before I knew it I was lost. It—it took me awhile to find my way back."

Rob said fiercely, "*Where* did thee get lost? Where?"

The shaking started again and this time she knew she couldn't stop it. She put her hands over her face to hide the tears that wouldn't stay behind her eyes. Mistress Teele came and gathered her close, making comfortable sounds while she stared over Deborah's head at Rob.

"This is no business of yours, Rob Bates," Mistress Teele said. "You be quiet."

"She's been up to no good. I think—"

"I've told you, Rob," Mistress Teele began, and got no further, for young Will pushed open the door and stood in it. His eyes were twice their normal size and his face was a grayish white. He spoke directly to Rob, as if there were no others in the room. "Come, Rob. *Hurry.* There's soldiers in the stable yard. *Hessian* soldiers. They're making ready to steal our hay and the master's away in the north field. Thee has got to stop them, Rob. Come *on!*"

Will's words seemed to turn Rob Bates into another person. His face lost its look of fanatic anger and hatred. His eyes, which had been wild and slightly out of focus when he had railed at Deborah, cleared and actually grew larger. He straightened his humped shoulders and walked briskly to the door. "I'll stop them, Will," he said, and Deborah, who had ceased her crying and lifted her head from Mistress Teele's shoulder as she listened to Will, could not believe this was the same boy who had, heretofore, appeared to be more than half demented.

"There's just a mistake, Will. Bound to be. We're loyal to the king. I'll just go along and put them right. Thee'd best stay here."

But Will wouldn't stay. He ran, a step or two behind Rob who didn't look back to see and stop him.

"I'd best go too," Mistress Teele said, and caught up a shawl from a chair back. Deborah gave Susannah a quick hug and said, "Back in a minute, small one," and left the kitchen.

The sun was setting as they got to the stable yard. They saw Rob Bates and a Hessian sergeant with half a dozen Hessian soldiers leaning on pitchforks, their conical hats picked out with points of the dying light, before they could hear any words. Will had stopped short of the rest and Mistress Teele took his shoulders and turned him toward the fields and said softly, "Run, Will. Run as fast as ever you can and fetch the master. I don't doubt we'll be needing him." When the boy was on his way she muttered to herself, "Much good it will do. He'll never get here in time."

The sergeant was speaking and they could hear now his slow, careful English words thick with the accent of his native Germany. "For the horses hay is needed yet. I will it take."

"But not from *us*," Rob Bates said, a hint of hysteric anger in the voice he was still at pains to keep, for the most part, reasonable and patient. "I told you. We're loyal to the British cause."

The sergeant shook his head and said to his men, "Achtung! Arbeiten Sie."

Deborah needed no interpreter of the strange words, for the men went immediately to the haymow and began to pitch hay into a cart one of them had already driven under the overhang of the stone barn.

Rob lost his carefully hoarded calm then and put his hands on the sergeant's shoulders and started to shake him, screaming, "Thee can't! Thee can't! Thee can't! We do be loyal subjects of the king I tell thee."

The sergeant was a giant of a man, tall and brawny. He was, besides, Deborah thought, infuriated by Rob's action and by his own inability to understand English when it was thus hurled at him. He reached up to Rob's oversize hands and wrenched them away as easily as if they had been Susannah's and gave Rob a violent push. Rob toppled over like one of Will's wooden soldiers. Arms flailing and legs flying out from under him, he fell backward and landed in a pile of steaming manure.

The sergeant grunted and straightened his mussed uniform and, taking a folded paper from his belt, threw it upon Rob's prostrate body. Then, ignoring the others as he had indeed done throughout the small scene, he directed his full attention to his men and the nearly finished work of loading the cart.

134

CHAPTER THIRTEEN

In spite of herself a small giggle, quickly smothered, escaped Deborah at the sight of Rob sprawled upon the manure pile like some giant insect. She thought she saw an answering gleam of amusement in Mistress Teele's face. But the situation was too serious for prolonged merriment. Rob's eyes were again bloodshot and crazed as he struggled out of his ignominy and started toward the Hessians. Dear Heaven, Deborah thought, he *is* bewitched. He's going to attack the whole lot of them and they will surely kill him.

Mistress Teele said, very quietly as if she were speaking to a child, "Bring me the paper, Rob."

Rob stopped and turned his head slowly toward her as if he were aware for the first time that she was present in the barnyard. He looked at her vacantly and shook himself, and the reek of manure, sharp with the smell of ammonia, stung Deborah's nose.

"Thee," he said after a second of staring. "I didn't know thee was here, Mistress."

"The paper, Rob. Pick it up and bring it to me."

Slowly, as if he were hypnotized and could do only as she bade him, he stooped and got the paper from the ground where it had fallen when he had hauled himself up and brought it to her.

"Now go to the house and cleanse yourself."

He shook his head and turned toward the barn where the cart stood almost full of hay. "Loyal," he said. "We're loyal. Must make him understand."

"Go to the house, Rob. It's all right. There's nothing more you can do here now. Leave it for the master. He is coming. I have sent for him. *Go to the house.*"

He stood a moment longer, his face shadowing the dazed state of his mind. Idly, his fingers brushed at the foul-smelling muck on his clothes though it was plain he had no consciousness of what he was doing. Then he turned slowly from them and broke into a half-run, lumbering toward the house with one arm shielding his face.

Mistress Teele let out her breath in a long sigh and looked at the paper she was holding.

"What is it?" Deborah asked, feeling weak with relief that Rob had been stopped from further entanglement with the Hessians.

"What I surmised—an order requisitioning hay. It is signed by General Knyphausen." Mistress Teele sent a look at the Hessians which would have killed them all if a look had power to kill. They had filled their cart and thrown their pitchforks atop the load and were lined upon either side ready to escort their stolen goods back to the city. "Gideon won't like it," Mistress Teele said, and watched the cart move away. When it was out of the stable yard she added very softly, though Deborah heard and could scarcely believe that she did, "Almost I wish McLane's Raiders would get them. Friends to us indeed!"

Too late, Gideon Teele came hurrying through the stubbled wheat with Will running to keep up with his long strides. "What is it? What's to do?" Gideon called to his wife while he was still a good way off.

She waited until he came up to them and handed

him the requisition and watched as he read it. Deborah expected him to explode into anger but he only asked mildly, "Who was in charge?" and when Mistress Teele answered, "Hessians," he said, "That likely explains it. Those poor homesick devils understand little English and less of the situation of this blasted war. No doubt the sergeant saw a good farm with likely hay at hand and helped himself without thought as to who owned it."

Mistress Teele said, "Rob tried to explain. The sergeant pushed him into the manure pile."

"Rob should have kept out of it. He's too—too distracted in his mind to undertake such responsibilities and I've told him so or tried to. Might have landed us all in a pickle."

"He did his best. You weren't here."

"But *you* were. The boy's got no judgment and too much anger."

"He's not like to trust a woman never having known one since his mother died when he was a baby. He did his best. Don't be too hard on him, Gideon."

"I'll not be too hard on him," Gideon said with a hint of impatience. "Have I ever been? But the boy's got to learn. I'll talk to him again. Now we'd best go in. It'll be full dark in a minute and I'm hungry besides. Tomorrow I'll go to British headquarters and get all this straightened out."

Gideon was already gone next morning when Deborah and a still shaky Susannah came down to breakfast. When he came home as they were about to sit at table for midday dinner his face was tight with pent-up anger and he had no greeting for any of them.

"What happened?" Mistress Teele asked anxiously.

"We'll eat first," her husband answered, and she nodded and they ate quickly, in silence, until the meal was done.

He pushed his chair back from the table then and spoke slowly and carefully as if he were afraid fury would choke the words in his throat. "I went straight to General Howe's headquarters. I saw the quartermaster himself and showed him Knyphausen's paper. I told him, quietly and reasonably mind you and not in anger, there must have been a mistake made, for we were no rebels and had not raised our hands and voices against King George."

He stopped, his face working, while a minute went by.

"And then?" Mistress Teele prompted when the silence was like to lay a burden on them all.

"He said—the quartermaster said, as bland as buttermilk—he said there'd been no mistake. They needed hay for the horses for even though the General's brother has cleared the river for the supply ships he brought no fodder for the beasts which must come from the land hereabouts. I would be paid for the hay, he said."

He hit the table with his fist and the dishes jumped and clattered. "Do you know what he offered me? Not half what the hay was worth. Not *half*. And when I protested he smiled a little, mocking smile and said since we were King George's loyal subjects we would not mind contributing the unpaid balance to His

Majesty's army that had come across the sea to protect us!"

He got up and began to walk up and down behind his chair, talking still, his voice getting louder and louder until he was shouting. "*Protect* us! Is this the way the English protect their friends? I tell you, Ruth, I've learned a thing this day. *All* colonials are the same to these English—*all* of us unless we be rich and powerful gentry, dancing and carousing with General Howe the nights through. They care no whit for us plain folk, though we be loyal even to our graves."

"*No!* It's not true!" The interruption came from Rob Bates, but Gideon paid him no more attention than if he had been a fly buzzing on a hot summer's day. Gideon sat down again in his chair and went on, a little more quietly, to his wife as if they two had been alone in the kitchen, "I'm thinking, Ruth, we've made a mistake about this War for Independence. I'm thinking we cannot stand aside from it, as we had hoped, and let those who want it so fight for freedom from England, but must commit ourselves to one side or the other. Likely the time has come when we must stand and be counted as either rebel or Tory, as staunch followers of General Washington or of General Howe. And I'm not liking the thought of hobnobbing and kowtowing as the Tories do to folk who'll steal as soon as kiss your hand—not after this day."

He stopped to draw breath and to go on with his thinking. Deborah sat very still, her mouth open a little. She had thought the Teeles *were* committed, had classed them with the Tories who sought in any way they could to throw down the Cause she believed in. She wondered whether Gideon Teele would change his mind again when the anger was gone and thought if he did not the British were indeed fools, for Gideon was a strong and forceful man and it would surely be better for General Howe to have him neutral than standing firmly behind the freedom fighters. He began again to speak and she turned her mind to listening.

"All men know that General Washington, though his needs are a thousand times greater than Howe's, will not let his men live off the land. And if *he* must take from us—even from farmers known to be against his cause—he pays in full. Maybe we've been wrong. Maybe it's true what the Virginian Jefferson wrote— maybe it's true it's time we stopped *being* colonials and 'assume, among the powers of the earth, the separate and equal station to which the Laws of Nature and of Nature's God entitle' us. Maybe we've been wrong, Ruth. Wrong and blind. Maybe this liberty's a thing important, a thing worth fighting for with all our souls."

He looked at her and she nodded and he said, "Think about it," and turned away from her and saw Rob standing before him, staring at him, his hands opening and closing in spasms of anguish. Deborah thought, Rob's going to throttle him, and held her breath as Gideon looked at the moving hands. "What's the matter with you, Rob? Why're you standing over me like that? Sit down, lad. Sit down, or better still get to work. There's wood to be chopped."

Deborah let out her breath. It would be all right.

Gideon could control Rob with just a look and she'd never known Rob to disobey an outright order.

But this time the magic didn't work. Rob stayed where he was and began to speak in a low, tense voice that was at once hurt and full of hate.

"It's not true what thee is saying. It's not true. They *are* our friends. They are if we stay loyal. Thee had betrayed them. Betrayed them when thee took a parcel of rebel brats into this house to treat better'n thee treats the—the rest of us. That one," he pointed to Deborah, "sneaking about to make trouble for the British with that tag-a-long Johnny Darragh. No wonder the Hessians take the hay. They'd be within their rights to pay thee nothing. Traitor!"

Gideon had gotten up from his chair again and he stood facing Rob, taller by a head and twice as heavy. The anger which had subsided a little while he talked of General Washington had returned to flush his face and mottle it. But he waited until Rob finished and then spoke reasonably, almost gently, as if to a small and naughty child.

"You don't know what you're saying, boy. Even if you were right in your thinking what could one small girl do to harm the British army? And do you think we're the only peaceable-minded farmers who've been robbed? I talked to near a dozen men this day. We've been lucky. Others are worse off than we. I know you've your own grievance against the Continental Congress, Rob, and I'm not saying you haven't cause to be hurt and angry, though I'm coming round to see there's two sides to the matter of the Virginia exiles. War's war and it's likely the innocent are bound to suffer with the guilty and those men were stubborn in their refusal to promise to stay neutral. Best you keep out of this, Rob, as I've told you before, else you'll bring trouble to all of us. Do you do your work and leave the thinking to me. And, Rob, I'll hear no more from you about my wife's cousins and their friend."

Now, Deborah thought, Rob will maybe leave me alone. But there was no holding him. He just stood a little taller and defied the man who had rescued him when his uncle was exiled.

"I'll not keep silent," he said. "I'll not. I'll not sit by and pretend all's well when there be rebels in this house." He sent such a look of hatred at Deborah she shivered in her chair.

"Rob! There's wood to be chopped."

This time there was no gentleness in Gideon Teele, only authority and menace and Rob recognized it. He got his coat and left the kitchen. But Deborah was not comforted. She thought he had taken all his hating for the men who had banished his uncle and transferred it to her and she knew he would harm her if he could. Harm her and Johnny.

The days that followed were rainy and miserable. The wet weather made it impossible to work in the fields and Rob was much in the house or about it. He didn't come near Deborah, didn't seem to look at her, but she knew he was, nonetheless, watching and biding his time, and she was careful not to be far from Mistress Teele or Annie. She thought he had likely guessed at her meetings with Johnny and hoped

143

to catch her going to one of them. So long, then, as Rob was not safely away from the house she would not go. Johnny would, she told herself, likely enough not come himself for a few days, not until his ankle had had a little time to mend itself. But she couldn't be sure. She knew very little about hurt ankles or about how long they took in their mending and she worried that he might come and think her faithless, or worse, afraid she might be asked to undertake another dangerous errand. No matter, she told herself, better risk his misunderstanding which could in time be explained away than have Rob sneaking after them, listening from some hideout to all they said.

Meantime she moped about the house while the rain poured sadly down outside. Mistress Teele moved, with worry and uncertainty as her companions, about her daily chores. Deborah guessed she was turning duty over in her mind, disturbed by the questions Gideon had raised about their loyalties. Only the recurring delight that she had been useful, in no matter how small a degree, to the cause of liberty lightened Deborah's gloom, and each night she prayed the sun would shine next day and Rob would be off and away from the house and she could meet Johnny.

During the last night of November the wind changed and the first of December came in a splendor of sparkling sunshine. At once the whole household brightened. Susannah's persistent cough that had followed her spell of the quinsy lessened and came only occasionally. Mistress Teele walked about with her old light step and smiled as if the fair wind had blown away her uncertainty with the rain clouds. Gideon took Rob and Will away to the very end of his land to clear a fallow field for spring plowing, and Deborah, with Susannah beside her, went singing down the lane.

And, wonder of wonders, Johnny was there, hobbling a little because his ankle was tight-bound with strips of linen cloth, but smiling and cheerful. For a few seconds everybody talked at once. Deborah and Johnny laughed at the babble and were quiet while Susannah, feeling important, told her brother how she'd got the quinsy and been put to bed and how Mistress Teele and Deborah had taken turns to keep her amused and happy. Johnny heard her out and made the proper responses, then sent her along the road a little to gather sprays of bittersweet that twined its orange-and-red berries among the low growth at the roadside.

When she was out of earshot he said, "I couldn't come before, Deborah," and at the same moment she said, "I was afraid you'd be angry with me that I didn't come," and they laughed again and linked their little fingers in the old spell against bad luck when two people speak at once. They laughed too because the day was perfect and they were companionable and each had feared needlessly for the other's good-will. Johnny explained that Lydia had thought he'd best rest his ankle for a few days, especially since there'd been no information to send to Charles in the button molds. He said Lydia had more than approved of his decision to tell Deborah their secret and sent her thanks for Deborah's help. She told him then all that had happened on her trip to the Rising Sun and afterward.

He looked distressed at her trouble with the sentry

but she made light of it, laughing as she described Jenkins' face when she had stuck her tongue out at him. Johnny was delighted at the probable change of heart of the Teeles. There were, he said, other Tory farmers who had been badly treated by the British and had switched their allegiance to the patriot cause. "And there'll be more. Old Howe's too arrogant to show sense; and his Hessians!" He clucked his tongue. "Thee'd not believe how stupid and cruel they can be. There are such tales—but I'll not take time to tell them."

"No," Deborah said. "Tell me instead how things go with the General. It's hard not knowing."

Johnny frowned. "He's settled the army at Whitemarsh and it's a good place, easily defended unless old Howe could manage to take him by surprise. For a time we hoped Washington would drive the British out of Philadelphia, but likely he thinks the time's not yet right, for his men are poorly clad and shod and more than a little hungry. So all's quiet in the town. Too quiet, Ma says. She thinks something's doing only none of us can find out just what. There's a deal of running about from Howe's headquarters to Cornwallis' to Knyphausen's but none can say the why of it. I wish we could find out something."

"Don't worry so, Johnny. You're doing all you can and nobody can do more than that, not even the angels. Besides you *said* there were many other watchers. Likely some of them will spy out something. Oh, I *wish* I could help again."

He patted her shoulder. "Thee's done enough, Deborah. Spying's no job for a girl."

"Your mother does it."

"Well, Ma's different. Besides she's old."

Deborah didn't see what age had to do with it. She wanted to argue but she saw he had put on his stubborn look and thought it would do no good. She made a face at him and he laughed and said, "Good old Deborah," which only irritated her.

Susannah came running back to them then, her arms full of color, and saved the afternoon that had begun so happily from ending in a quarrel.

Johnny hugged his small sister and gave her a sweetmeat he'd been saving in his pocket. "Come each sunny day, then, Deborah," he said. "I'll wait as long as I can in case thee has trouble with that Rob, drat him!" He dropped his voice to a whisper and gestured toward Susannah who had already started toward the lane. "Best leave the little one with Cousin Ruth whenever thee can."

His suggestion made Deborah feel better. Even if she couldn't go on as an active part of General Washington's spy net it seemed clear Johnny expected to have secrets to tell her, secrets he didn't want Susannah to overhear. At least then he didn't intend to shut her out from his confidences. She'd have to be content with that.

CHAPTER FOURTEEN

By the next day the wind had shifted again and brought one of those rare, deceptive, mild December days that tantalize because they hint at spring, still weary months of a cold and frozen world in the future. Deborah had managed to slip away from Susannah and waited alone at the lane's end for Johnny. Nothing moved in any direction on the long road. From a dark grove of trees at a little distance a flock of crows quarreled among themselves. Their raucous cawing was unfriendly and served only to accentuate the loneliness that seemed to Deborah to have seized hold upon her spirit. She had the feeling she had been wrenched out of her place and time; that she was the only human being in an alien land. She shivered in spite of the balmy breeze that, a moment before, had caused her to open her cloak.

She had, she guessed, been waiting half an hour and she wondered what was keeping Johnny. Was his ankle worse? Had (Heaven forbid it!) he or Lydia been suspected in their spying and taken by the British? Or, worse, had Rob Bates, unknown to her, followed her yesterday and overheard their talk and managed to warn someone at General Howe's headquarters? She shook her shoulders, telling herself not to be a ninny. Hadn't she questioned young Will last night when they went up to bed and hadn't he assured her Rob had not been the whole day out of his sight?

Something moved in the thicket behind her and she jumped, sure Rob *had* followed her this time. If he had he'd not hear anything for she'd leave at once. But she'd best make sure. Moving quietly and cautiously she went to investigate and found a rabbit crouched with his back to her as if the silly creature thought itself unseen because it could not see its enemy. She laughed, a little shakily, at her own fears and said *"Boo!"* and watched the small animal leap twice its own length to escape.

"Stupid," she called after it, eager to hear a voice even if it was only her own, "I'd not harm you."

She thought Johnny was surely not coming. She'd best get back to Susannah before the child called undue attention to her absence. She took a final look up the road and saw Johnny, limping still but hurrying as fast as he could. Even at a distance she could tell he was excited and she went a little way up the road to meet him. He came up to her and when she would have turned back toward the lane stopped her.

"Best stay in the middle of the road," he said. "That way we can be sure no one's hiding to hear us. And speak quietly, Deborah. Is thee *sure* Rob Bates is not about?"

"Sure as I can be," she said and told him about the rabbit. Curiosity filled her mind at his caution. "Why? What's happened to make you fear Rob's coming today?"

He went a little way in each direction prying into the growth on each side of the road, making sure no other ears were listening. When he began to talk he, nevertheless, kept his voice so low she had almost to strain to hear him.

"We've found out, Deborah. We've *found out* what's been going on. And it's as we thought. Old Howe's planning a surprise attack on the army at Whitemarsh!"

"Johnny! But that's—that's . . ." She could not go on. She was afraid to put into words the thoughts of disaster to the General and his army, of danger to Uncle Matt, that were running through her mind.

"I know," Johnny said. "If old Howe should catch the

149

General, should kill or capture his men, it would likely be the end—the very end of all our hopes for freedom."

"Not the end, Johnny!" This was worse than her own mind had conjured. "There are other soldiers, aren't there? Thousands of them north and south of us?"

"Yes, Deborah. But doesn't thee see? The General's men are the heart of the whole army. We're right in the middle, holding the British, keeping them from getting together, keeping old Howe tied down. If he destroys the General's army the rest will be separated from each other. They could be—*picked off*, one after one, as easy as picking apples off a tree. Besides, where would we be without the General?"

"Oh, Johnny!" she whispered, not able to say anything further.

"*Listen!* All's not lost. Ebenezer got word to us yesterday the General's been warned about what's brewing. Trouble was nobody knew exactly how or when old Howe expected to move. Then, last night, when we'd just finished our supper, a redcoat officer came and told Ma they'd be wanting to use the front room. They've used it a time and a time before but this was different. He told Ma—the officer did—the whole family must be abed by seven of the clock. She was to make up the fire and leave the door unlatched and on no account were any of us to come belowstairs until the redcoats were gone. He would, he said, come himself to tell her when they had all left."

He stopped to swallow and catch breath, for he'd been talking fast and intently. In the moment's pause she asked, "Why would they want to use your front room, Johnny? Don't they have plenty of room at their own headquarters?"

He shook his head impatiently. "*I* don't know, Deborah. Likely old Howe wants to keep his whole house for the levees and dinners and balls and routs he flatters his Tory friends with. And amuses himself to boot, no doubt. I'm telling you *what* happened, not why. Anyway we all scurried upstairs like herded goats and went to our rooms soon as the officer left. I heard the tramping when the redcoats came in and then I got in my bed and put the pillow over my head for it made me angry having them there and I didn't want to hear more of them. I must have been tireder than I knew because I went to sleep and slept the whole night through. But Ma didn't."

He stopped again, like a storyteller adding suspense to his tale and she said, "Go *on*, Johnny. Go on. What did your Ma do?"

"She pretended to go to bed. But instead, when the hall was quiet and the door of the front room shut with the British inside, she got up and stole down the back stairs and crept into the cupboard in the kitchen that backs against the wall of the room where the men were. Does thee remember it?"

She nodded.

"For some reason Mr. Loxley, the man who built our house a time ago, made that wall thinner than the rest and in the cupboard you can hear everything said on the other side. Ma listened and memorized what she heard. She knows it all, Deborah. All old Howe's plans. When he'll go and how many men and how many guns. Everything!"

"Johnny!" Her eyes which had been sparkling with delight clouded suddenly with anxiety for Lydia. "Did she get away clear, your Ma?"

"That she did, and fooled the British altogether, to boot." He laughed briefly at the recollection of his mother's cleverness.

"*Tell* me."

"When she was sure she had it all—all the General would need—she went back to her room and got into bed again. Not above five minutes later the British officer came and knocked on her door. She didn't move, just lay there pretending to snore until he had knocked three more times, each time louder than the last. Then she went to the door, yawning and looking sleepy, and he told her they were leaving and she'd best shake herself awake long enough to lock up after them and see to the fire. He said he wished *he* could sleep so soundly."

"So now what's she going to do?" Deborah asked, eager to know the whole plot.

Johnny's face lengthened. "She won't tell me. Honest she won't. She's making preparations to do *something*. I'm sure of that for she found errands for all of us away from the house, even Pa. She says nobody should know her plans. But, before I went away at her bidding, she said she was worried."

"Worried? And well she might be."

"Yes, but it's not as thee thinks. It's not for herself."

"What, then?"

"Well, she's going to carry her message to *somebody*. I'm sure of that. So suppose she's stopped or turned back once she's started. It's not likely the British will fail to be extra cautious right now. Suppose they won't accept her pass. Then what will happen to the warning? She can't get it out with Ebenezer, for he sent word the British told him to keep out of the city with his vegetables for them for the next few days. So she needs a second string to her bow and she says it can't be me. She says I couldn't run fast enough if I needed to run because of this dratted ankle. And besides two Darraghs roaming about the countryside might cause suspicion and that would ruin our usefulness for the future."

He looked so woebegone, Deborah could have laughed if she hadn't felt so sorry for him. She knew how he must feel. Worse even than *she* did, because she couldn't go on spying for the General. After all, he'd done so much more than she, he'd think he was a real and permanent part of all his mother's planning and . . . Some part of her mind snapped into place and she said, *"Johnny!"* Excitement sent her voice up and he looked around and warned her to quiet: "Sh-h-h. *Quietly*, Deborah."

She thought him overcautious in the large loneliness of the countryside but she obeyed his warning and whispered. *"I* can do it. I can be the second string."

"Don't be silly. Of course thee can't." He sounded almost sulky.

"Why? Why can't I? I wouldn't have to pass out of the city because I'm *already* out so none of the guards could stop me. I could go to the Rising Sun as I did before."

"And that's the very reason thee cannot go again."

"But why? I can ask for your brother. That sentry's

not like to refuse me again. Not after Charles let me in before."

"Thee *is* a ninny, Deborah. The same man likely won't be on sentry duty again, girl. And I don't think Charles will be there either. McLane's men won't be hanging about the tavern now. They'll be watching all the possible roads that lead to Whitemarsh."

"Well, *somebody'll* be there."

"And thee ought to know," he went on as if she hadn't interrupted him, "thee ought to know they'll not let a *girl* in. Not without Charles to tell them to."

"They needn't even know I'm a girl."

"Oh *needn't* they? And why not? They have eyes, don't they?"

"Wait," she said, and turned from him and scooped up a handful of dust from the ground and rubbed it over her face. She hunched her shoulders and twisted her face into the seeming of an old, old woman. Her hands, long and slim and graceful, crooked themselves until they became knobby claws and she turned to him again holding them out and saying in a high, thin whine, "Please, kind sir, alms—alms for an old woman who's had nothing to eat these three days past."

He stared at her, seeing not only the physical transformation but some inner change as if she had thought herself into the role of an ancient crone. He laughed softly and said, "Deborah, I wouldn't know thee. Thee looks about eighty. It might work. It just might. Now let's think. Thee couldn't go begging. They might give thee a crust of bread but they'd never let thee in."

"Maybe I could pretend to have something to sell."

"Um-m-m. Maybe. I'd best ask Ma."

154

Deborah didn't, upon consideration, think her new idea much better than the old. But that didn't worry her. Once there she'd find a way of getting inside. The thing to do now was to convince Johnny to let her go. Quickly, before he could see the flaws in her new suggestion, she said, "But I'll need some clothes, Johnny. Some kind of disguise. Maybe I don't look like myself in the face but I'd hardly fool anybody if I put an old face on these." She gestured to her neat blue cloak and well-shined boots. "And I haven't anything that would do for an old woman. I could ask Mistress Teele maybe, but I'm not that sure her new-found loyalty to our cause would go as far as helping us spy."

"No," he agreed. "Best not let Cousin Ruth know. And besides there's too many people in this already. Fewest knows, least chance for failure. But don't worry. I'm sure Ma can fix thee something."

"But there's no *time*," she wailed. "No time to get clothes from your ma and bring them to me."

"Yes, there is. Just. Old Howe won't move until the day after tomorrow. And I'm sure Ma isn't planning anything for today. She needs time to make her own arrangements. Now let's see. Could thee manage somehow to be here before daylight tomorrow morning? Well before daylight?"

"Yes, of course." She didn't know how, but she would manage. "But how will you get out of the city in the dark? The guards at the road will never let you pass."

"I know a way. Through an old root cellar that will bring me out beyond the guard post. I used to play there when I was little. It's a tight squeeze and well

155

overgrown now but I can still just manage it. I'll be here."

"But what will I tell them at the Rising Sun?"

"Best wait on that till I come tomorrow. And watch out for that Rob. If he should find out . . ."

"He won't. If there's any danger of that I'll not come. Trust me to have a *little* sense, Johnny."

"I do trust thee," he said. "There's only one thing. If Ma says no, we'll have to give the whole thing up."

Deborah was, on the instant, sobered; the excitement that had been with her while they planned gone as completely as if it had never been. Lydia *would* say no. She was sure of it. Lydia would think her too young or too foolish or not fit because she was a girl. Or Lydia would think the risk too great for her to run. She saw her chances for doing a really important thing for General Washington gone with a decision she could have no part in influencing.

"Oh, Johnny," she said, and made the words a prayer, "don't let her say no. Don't *let* her."

He said quickly and soberly, "She knows best, Deborah. We'll have to bide by her word. And see here. My pa says sometimes a body can help most by doing least. It's the willingness to do whatever is needed that counts. Even if thee is asked to do—nothing. He says some old blind English poet wrote about that. How did it go? Yes, that's it. 'They also serve who only stand and wait.' Thee'd surely not want to risk ruining everything just to satisfy thine own importance."

"No," she said, rebuked but not hurt, for she saw he was just. "You're right, Johnny. I'll do whatever Lydia thinks best. But *oh* I hope she won't say I can't go because she fears the danger for me."

"That she won't do, Deborah. I'm sure Ma believes this—this liberty we're fighting for is more important than any of us, not just the soldiers and officers in the army. No, I'm sure she'll say for thee to go if it's best for—for General Washington and the men under him. Best get back now. Thee has been a long time gone. Here," he handed her his kerchief. "Wipe the dust away."

She did as he told her before she went, slowly, a little sadly, for his words had reminded her that what they had planned was not a lark thought up for her entertainment or the satisfaction of her pride. The lives of thousands of men could depend upon warning the General about the exact nature of Howe's plan for the surprise attack; upon getting the warning safely through without raising any British suspicions.

Her eyes widened as she realized how much responsibility she might be carrying tomorrow. If Lydia should be stopped, or turned back before she gave her message to—to somebody, somebody who would send it on to General Washington, then everything would depend upon Deborah Stone, fifteen years old and a girl. *If* Lydia agreed she should be the needed second string.

Almost she hoped Lydia would say no. For suppose she, too, tried and failed. She had no notion that it would be easy to get into the Rising Sun. She didn't for one minute believe any sentry would let any old woman wander around loose in what she guessed was the headquarters for the General's spies. And she couldn't plan ahead what she would do, even if she had had any experience in spying. She couldn't foresee what circumstances she would meet once she was there. And she'd almost failed before. Without the intervention of Charles Darragh . . . Still she had learned something from that first trip. She had learned about the sentries. This time she'd have to depend upon some inspiration to get her inside, for she knew argument wouldn't work. Depression settled upon her. She didn't think she was very good at inspiration. Nothing in her life had prepared her to make quick decisions. She wished she hadn't started this; wished she had had the sense to be satisfied with her one little bit of spying.

Suppose Rob caught her!

The thought of him stiffened her drooping spirits. He became for her suddenly the symbol of the whole British army, of all the tyrannies of King George Uncle Matt had told her of. Just let Rob Bates try to stop her. He'd get nothing out of her. No matter what he did. If Lydia would let her carry this message—this all important message—she'd do it. One way or another and no matter what the difficulties.

She straightened her shoulders and hurried her lagging steps toward the house where Susannah was waiting in the yard under the stark branches of the stripped maples.

CHAPTER FIFTEEN

Deborah did not again let her mind slip into fear or despair. Nor did she spend any time wondering about Lydia's decision. She would proceed as if she were sure she would go to the Rising Sun and plan as best she could toward that end. Carefully, she listed in her mind, under neat headings, the preparations she must make:

Getting to the tavern. She thought she had best avoid the public road and sent her memory back along the way Charles Darragh had brought her through the woods when he had ridden her home from her other journey into danger. At first the picture of the path would not come and she thought this was, perhaps, because she was trying to see it all at once. She cleared her mind and started again, working backward from the moment when he had said, "Two minutes will see you home," and reviewed, a bit at a time, the whole way they had come and found she could recall enough small landmarks to guide her.

Susannah. She would have to make sure Susannah was sleeping too soundly to waken and question her when she went to get her disguise. That shouldn't be difficult. She had only to keep the child up later than usual by an hour or more telling her stories, and Susannah would be so deep in sleep she'd not know anything was amiss.

The Teeles. Their room was at the front of the house. Gideon Teele was, she knew, a noisy sleeper. His loud and regular snores would cover any small noise she might make if she went out by the back stairs. Annie would not be about, for she went to her home to sleep.

Rob Bates. He was the only real problem. She had no idea whether his sleeping was deep or light. And the back door she planned to use was hard by his little room. She could not, she decided, plan ahead for him. She could only trust to luck and have an extra care for quiet when she unlatched the door.

Then, almost at the last minute, chance removed the problem of Rob. One of the plough team was showing signs of distemper, and Rob, who in spite of his wildness had a way with animals, planned to sleep beside the horse in the stable.

That left to be considered only the matter of getting into her disguise and away with the message later in the day. She could cover her actual preparations and the trip to the tavern by claiming a headache that could be cured only with rest. The Woman (Deborah smiled to herself to think she would twice bless her memories of the Woman!)—the Woman had often had such severe pains in her head she'd been forced to spend hours in a darkened room till they abated a little. Deborah remembered all the Woman's symptoms and was sure she could imitate them.

Further than that she could not see. And perhaps it was better so, for if she had no plan for what she would do at the Rising Sun there would be no plan to go wrong. She took Susannah up to bed with a quiet mind, delighted the child with story after story, and saw her drop into sleep as a stone drops into a deep pool. Then she lay down herself, completely dressed, upon the big bed. She dozed a little through the long night but she did not really sleep. She was terrified she might not awake in time to be at the road before dawn and the tension of her fear roused her quickly each time her eyes closed. When she judged the time was right, she got up and wrapped her cloak about her and went softly down the stairs.

Three-quarters of the way down a tread creaked, the

sound loud as gunfire. She froze, as the rabbit had frozen; and stood, all her life seeming to be concentrated in her ears, listening for an answering sound from the sleeping house. Nothing stirred, no one called out. Then the grandfather clock in the front hall wheezed and began to strike and, under cover of its bonging, she fled the rest of the way down and eased open the door and knew she had completed the first part of her plan safely.

She ran around the house and all the way down the lane, stumbling sometimes in the dark, and found Johnny already waiting at its end. She saw, at once, the dark bundle at his feet and knew, without surprise, that Lydia had agreed to her going. Yesterday she would have been filled with jubilation. Now she felt nothing except the need to hear what Johnny had to say and get back to the house before the rising sun wakened the family.

Neither she nor Johnny wasted time in idle talk. He took from his pocket an old, dirty case for keeping needles. It was made of some black cloth frayed around the edges and was small enough to hide in the hand. He unrolled it and, by the graying dawn she saw four little pockets sewed into the lining. From the last of these pouches Johnny took a bit of paper, tight rolled like the stem of a clay pipe, and showed her a message written upon it.

"Memorize it," he said, "so if thee has to rid thyself of the paper, thee'll remember the words."

She read the message three times and repeated it to him without looking at the paper. It said, "Howe will come to Whitemarsh tomorrow with 5000 men, 13 pieces of cannon, baggage wagons, 11 boats on wheels."

She said, "I'll remember it just as it's set down." A part of her mind wondered about the boats but she would not take time to ask about that now.

Johnny, his face tight, said, "If—if thee should meet a redcoat, *get rid of it.*"

She wanted to ask "How?" but she saw how nervous he was and only nodded. She thought he would not be jumpy if he were going himself but he had little confidence in her: likely would have had as little in anybody else. She said, "Stop worrying, Johnny."

"Thee—thee is different today. Thee are sure thee wants to go? Thee is not—not afraid?"

She considered her answer a second, then gave it honestly. "Reckon I am, a little. Reckon anybody would be. Anybody with sense. But I'll go. Being afraid's just a thing in your mind. You don't have to let it stop you from doing what you know has got to be done."

She put the needlebook in the pocket of her cloak, picked up the bundle of clothes, said, "It will be sunup directly. I'd best get on with it. Just don't you worry. I'll get the message to the Rising Sun."

He touched her arm and said, "Good luck, Deborah. The Lord keep thee," and turned away abruptly and hobbled toward the town, not looking back.

By the time the first slim fingers of rose red and saffron yellow reaching up from the horizon heralded the coming day Deborah was undressed, lying straight in her bed pretending sleep, and in a fidget for Susannah to wake up and find her so. But she had done her work well the night before. The child slept on and it was Deborah who had, in the end, to do the wakening. She began at once to try on her pretense of pain. When Susannah, noticing, said, "What's the matter, Deborah? Thy forehead's all wrinkled up," she answered, "It's no matter, Suzy. Only my head hurts some."

Susannah accepted the explanation without comment but, as Deborah had hoped, they were no sooner downstairs than the youngster announced, "Deborah's head hurts, poor thing."

Mistress Teele took immediate charge. "I wonder what could be the matter?" she said. She felt Deborah's forehead and added, "No fever. Best eat something."

Deborah said, "It's nothing, Mistress. Just a little hurt. It will go away." But she managed to look as if she were indeed ravaged with pain.

"Nonsense," Mistress Teele said. "It's plain to see you're suffering. When you've finished your breakfast you're to go straight back to bed. Susannah, you'll get your dolls and anything else you're likely to want for the whole day. I'll keep an eye on the child, Deborah, and see she doesn't disturb you. What you need is hours of quiet and rest. Sleep if you can. Nothing like sleep to mend an ailing head. Shall I come up and draw the curtains? No. Well, if you've done with your food, get along with you. Nobody will come near you this day unless you call."

Deborah made herself walk slowly up the stairs, holding to the rail as if each step sent an answering throb through her body. Susannah ran ahead and passed her coming down again with her playthings. "I'm sorry, Deborah," she said. "I'll be good and give Aunt Ruth no trouble. I promise." The child looked so distressed that, for a moment, Deborah hated her deceit and the need for it. Then Susannah scampered away and Deborah reached the top of the stairs where she would not be seen and dropped her simulation of pain. She forgot everything except the need to do what she must and went to her room and shut the door firmly behind her and, as a precaution, locked it.

Quickly she took off her dress and got the bundle from the chest where she had hidden it when she came in. The outside of the bundle proved to be a tattered cloak, so old it was impossible to guess what its color had been. Wrapped inside were a baggy gray dress and a pair of boots that must at some distant time have belonged to a boy. The uppers were broken and holed but the soles, she noticed gratefully, were sound.

She put on the clothes and almost giggled at herself in them. But there was no time for laughter. She went to the fireplace and collected the ashes scattered on the hearth and propped her mirror where the light would catch it. She mixed the ashes with water from the ewer and sat studying her face in the mirror, twisting it this way and that, thinking of a time when Uncle Matt had taken her to the playhouse to visit a friend he had made upon his journeys. The friend was a young man, an actor, and he was making himself ready to play his part which was to be an elderly gentleman. While he talked to Uncle Matt he transformed his face to fit the character and Deborah had watched fascinated as he worked. Now she took a little time to remember what he had done before she began upon her own face. When she had remembered what she could of his actions she set to work, watching her face in the mirror, and rubbed the grayish mixture of ashes and water into her skin until her normal, healthy color was well hidden. When her whole face was covered with the paste she went to the fireplace again and found a bit of charred stick spewed out from last night's burning, and cold. She rubbed her fingers well with the black from the stick and screwed her face into the lines of an old woman and carefully rubbed the black into them, on her forehead and cheeks and around her eyes and mouth. When she was done she inspected herself, thought the lines too stark and unnatural and got more dry ashes to powder them. Her neck, she decided, still looked too young and she found an old kerchief in the chest and dirtied it with the rest of the ashes and twisted it about her throat and inside the neck of the dress.

She would, she decided, do.

She wondered where best to hide the needlebook. It should be in a place where it would not show in case she met anyone upon her way but also where it could be easily disposed of if that need arose. She could thrust it down her dress. But then she'd likely be hard put to rid herself of it. The same thing would be true of one of her shoes, and besides she wanted nothing that might slow her walking—or running if that should be necessary. She examined the ancient cloak and found it had a good, deep pocket and decided that, being the simplest, would probably be the best hiding place. She thrust the needlebook deep inside, saw it made no bulge in the already sagging material, found she could get at it and hide it in her fist or even in her mouth easily enough, tied the bonnet string under her chin, and was ready.

By force of habit she picked up her own gloves and felt a warning prick in her mind and dropped them as if they had burned her hand. No old crone would be wearing neatly knitted, holeless gloves. She'd have to bear with the cold and she must remember to dirty her hands when she was outside.

She went to the door and had her hand on the key when her mind pricked again in warning and she stopped aghast. In all her planning yesterday she hadn't once thought how she was going to get out. Here she was, ready to start her momentous journey, trapped in her own room. And three people downstairs stood between her and escape from the house.

She knew the morning routine. Mistress Teele would certainly be moving about in the front room with the door wide open, doing her daily stint of dusting and polishing, barring Deborah from the front door. And Annie and Susannah would be in the kitchen so she could not gain the back exit unseen. What was she to do?

On her tiptoes lest the floor boards creak and show her to be still out of her bed, she went to the window and parted the curtains a crack. A slate roof that covered the stillroom and Rob's cubicle slanted steeply outside. A maple tree, old and sturdy, grew at the side and thrust one heavy branch actually onto the roof. If she could get to the branch she might make her way down the tree even in the cumbersome skirts that hampered her legs. *If* she could get to the branch. It looked a mile away. She shuddered at the steep cant of the slates. But she *must* reach the branch. And she must trust nobody would see her on the roof or in the tree. She had no notion where Rob was. She had not dared ask. For all she knew he might come out of the stable at any moment and look up and see her. If he caught her—if anyone caught her . . . She tore her mind away from that *if*. She had a chance. Once upon the roof she could spy out the land and, if necessary, withdraw before she was caught. If only she were not so terrified at the thought of those steeply slanting slates and the ground infinitely far below them. Whispering, she admonished herself, "Remember how you boasted to Johnny. Fear's only in your mind. It needn't keep you from doing what you must do. And this thing I must do, for I promised."

She took a deep breath to quiet the fluttering that was beginning inside her and slipped behind the curtains. Slowly, carefully, inch by cautious inch, she raised the sash until she could crawl beneath it, then, as slowly, closed it again. She peered along the roof to the ground and her head began to swim and she closed her eyes for a moment. When she opened them again she was careful not to look further than her feet. One thing at a time. Don't think even one second ahead. Take each step as it comes and do it. She crouched down upon the slates and crept forward toward the branch, praying she would not lose her nerve or her equilibrium.

Her progress seemed to her to be agonizingly slow. The branch, when she risked another look toward it, seemed as many miles away as ever, but the look restored a little of her confidence for, bent over as she was, her eyes were nearly on a level with the roof and she no longer felt the dizziness that had almost overcome her earlier. She moved a little faster, and, after a moment or two, felt the branch actually scratch at her hand, and grasped it firmly, and risked a glance out and down. The yard and outbuildings were empty as if this bustling farm were in fact deserted. She wished she could stay thus anchored in safety for a few minutes, just long enough to assess the fear that had been tearing at her and be rid of it. But who could say how soon someone might come into the empty spaces below and look up and see her? She had no time to wait. She got to her feet and tucked the awkward skirts into the dress belt and eased herself out upon the branch. It cracked ominously but it held her weight and she crawled along it to another, lower limb and so from limb to limb until she was close enough to the ground to risk swinging free and letting go.

She landed on her hands and knees, unhurt. She remembered to rub her hands in the dirt beneath the tree until they looked as filthy as the rest of her. Then she was up and hugging the house wall until she could make a dash across the corner of the still mercifully empty stable yard to the security of a thick copse of pines beyond.

CHAPTER SIXTEEN

She stopped long enough to let down her skirts before she took the path that would lead her into the larger woodland, and so, eventually, to the Rising Sun Tavern. She walked steadily for a quarter of an hour, forcing herself to forget her scrambling escape from her room and think only of the task ahead.

The path, no doubt begun a long, long time ago by wandering animals, ambled lazily with many twists and turns. As she came around an angle she saw Rob Bates coming toward her. He was the last person she had feared to meet here but she had no time to wonder where he had been. Fortunately his head was down and she had the chance to set her face in the lines of age and her hands into claws before a twig snapped as she trod upon it and the sound caught his attention. He lifted his head and stared at her, scowling, and she felt panic rise in her. He was going to speak to her. He was, she could see, already suspicious; whether of her or of any stranger who might be upon the path she had no way of knowing. But suspicion would likely sharpen his ears. It was one thing to fool someone who didn't know her with her aged whine. But Rob was familiar with each tone of her voice and she couldn't be sure whether or not she could change it enough to satisfy a real and searching curiosity sharpened by half-crazed doubts.

She had the wit to keep walking in the hobbling step she'd decided to use, pretending to pay no attention to him. He had stopped and barred the path and she made to go around him into the brush at its side, hoping to avoid speech, but he reached out and clutched her shoulder with one of his great hands, hurting her so she almost cried out.

"Who be thee? What is thee doing on this path, old dame?"

At least he hadn't seen beneath her disguise, she thought, and with the thought came inspiration. She shook her head and pointed first to her ears and then to her mouth and made a gabbling sound in her throat.

"Answer me!" he shouted, and threatened her with an upraised arm.

She cowered away from him, genuinely afraid of what he might do, and desperately repeated her dumb show.

He dropped his arm slowly and a look of pity changed his whole face until she could almost have liked him. "Deaf and dumb, is it?" he said. "Poor creature. Get along with thee then and may the Lord have mercy upon thee." He stepped out of the path and she went past him, glad that another turn would hide her quickly.

She met no one else upon the way, though once, warned by the clop-clop of a horse, she hid herself behind a clump of bushes and watched, her heart thumping with fear, as a lone British soldier rode by. She stayed where she was, shaking at the near encounter, wondering if others were behind him, for a good ten minutes before she could gather courage to go on. But there were no more alarms.

As she came around a final twist of the path and saw the dark bulk of the tavern against the sun, she reset her face and hands and body into the guise of age and moved, hobbling, toward the Rising Sun. Her mind was working quickly now, freed from its laggard fears by the time for action. She had, she thought, best reconnoiter the place before she tried to get into it. She remembered a hedge of laurels that bordered the side of the inn. If she could squeeze between them and the house wall she could likely get a look into the window of the room she'd been in before. The way to the hedge was protected from the stable yard by a picket of horses ready saddled, their heads in feed bags. She passed them quietly, without disturbing their placid feeding, and gained the laurels. She was right. There was a narrow corridor between them and the house and she crept along it, unconscious of the scratches the reaching twigs made on her hands and face, until she came to the window she remembered. Standing tiptoe, she could see inside where a group of men were just sitting down to a table upon which a meager meal had been set out. She didn't know who they were but she thought it mattered little. If she could just get into that room she'd find a way of passing on her message. She put her hand in the pocket of the old cloak and touched the needlebook as if it had been a talisman to bring her safely within the tavern. She eased along the narrow way until she came to the angle of the building. Peeping around it she could see the sentry on duty—not Jenkins but another, as Johnny had foretold—standing stiff and erect not three feet from her.

She stooped over and examined the ground at her feet, not knowing what exactly she planned but acting upon some instinct that seemed to tell her what to do. She straightened with a large rock in her hand. Sure that only the one sentry was before the inn she took careful aim and threw the stone so that it landed yards away and to the right of the door. It made a satisfactorily loud thud. Startled, the sentry looked toward the place where the rock had fallen, and, after a second, shouldered his musket and went to investigate.

Deborah had already gathered the cumbersome skirt into her hand and, as the sentry moved, she ran, lightly and quietly. She gained the door and was through it before the man, shaking his head, turned back to his place.

She'd gained the first advantage!

The hall was empty and she crossed it, thinking a prayer of thanksgiving that this part of her venture was successfully completed. She opened the remembered door into the room where Charles Darragh had interrogated her. Half a dozen pairs of eyes turned to her in astonishment. Surprise gave her a moment of time and she circled the table quickly to the man who sat at its head. She guessed he was the leader since he was older and held the place of honor. But before she could speak to him the younger men erupted into words.

"Who are you?"

"What are you doing here?"

"How did you get in?"

"Where's that blasted sentry?"

The babble of questions startled her and left her mind confused. Horrified, she heard herself speak words that were, in the circumstances, meaningless; words that had come into her mind no doubt from the time Johnny had babbled of the mill at Frankford when he was in just such another spot of fear and confusion. She was relieved—though a little surprised—that her voice was the voice of the old woman she was pretending to be. "The mill," she said. "Permission to go to the mill."

None of the younger men paid any attention to the words. One of them pushed back his chair and came toward her, speaking roughly, "You get out of here, old crone. You've no—"

Before he finished, the big, florid man at the head of the table spoke. "Leave her be, Lieutenant." He had not taken his eyes from her and she was sure *he* had heard the nonsense about the mill. Almost it seemed to have some special meaning for him. He said to her, courteously enough, "What is it? What do you want?"

Still confused, she turned to face him. "I do be needing flour," she said, wanting time to straighten her thoughts and having just enough wit to stick to her earlier babble. "May I go to the mill, please, your honor?"

He smiled thinly. "You don't need my permission for that. *We're* not set to harass innocent folk. Go along then when you like."

The small respite was enough. She saw her way clear. She took the needlebook from her pocket and held it out to him. The lieutenant who had tried to turn her out grabbed for it but, again, the large man stopped him. "But, General Budinot," the lieutenant said, and Deborah's heart jumped with relief, for she knew that name, had heard this General Budinot was close to General Washington, "we don't know who she is. There may be some danger in this."

"Sit down, Lieutenant. The danger, if indeed there is any, had already been done when she got by the sentry. That thing she's holding is nothing but a bit of cloth, albeit a filthy one. And she's no more than a little, poor-looking, insignificant old woman. There's nothing

174

to fear in this. You are too jumpy by far." He reached out and took the needlebook and turned it over in his hand. His intelligent eyes held a gleam, whether of amusement or expectation Deborah couldn't say.

"A penny, kind sir," she whined. "Please to give me a penny for my pretty needlebook. For the flour. A penny for a poor old woman who would buy a bit of flour."

She was beginning to enjoy herself and thought she could go on embroidering on the errant theme indefinitely if need be. The men around the table were laughing at her. They had been soothed by the General's air of casual unconcern and had lost their suspicions of her. They may have wondered how she had got in but they were obviously not worrying about it now, thinking her no more than the half-witted woman she was pretending to be. One of them said, "You can take it home, a present for your wife, General, when the war's over."

General Budinot took no notice of the chaffing. "It may be I *will* give you a penny, good woman. But not now. See, you have interrupted our dinner and we're all more than a little hungry. Leave me your needlebook. Go now and come again when I've had time to examine it. Tom, show the lady out through the kitchen."

One of the young men got up and made her a mocking bow and led her out by the back door. Once outside she scuttled for the laurel screen again and found the window and looked in. General Budinot had the needlebook in his hands. He had unrolled it and was going through the pockets. As she watched he came

to the last one and found the rolled paper and read it.
Though she could hear no words his face showed satisfaction and concern and excitement. At once, one of
his aides ran out of the room and in a moment she
heard him calling excitedly for the General's horse.
She retraced her way behind the shield of horses and
gained the wood path, triumphant. The message would,
she was sure, be on its way to General Washington
in minutes. If Lydia had gotten through it would do
no harm that the General would be twice warned. If
Lydia had been stopped it wouldn't matter, for word
of Howe's plans would reach Whitemarsh in ample time
for General Washington to make detailed and adequate
preparations. The surprise attack would, in any case,
be bound to fail.

Her feet fairly flew over the twisting path. She
crossed the corner of the stable yard unseen and was
up the tree and over the roof and through the window
without a thought of fear. She stripped off the bedrag-
gled clothes and remade them into a bundle and hid
them and washed the grime from her face and hands
and remembered to unlock the door. She was, suddenly,
overwhelmingly exhausted and she had no more than
fallen upon the big bed before her eyes closed and
she was as deep in sleep as Susannah had been the
night before.

Deborah slept the night through. Though she had
had nothing to eat since breakfast, hunger failed to
disturb her at suppertime. She didn't know that Mistress Teele came in and looked at her and went away

again, nor did the candle Susannah carried when she came to bed waken her.

No one seemed surprised at her long sleep when she came down to breakfast the next morning, only pleased to hear her head no longer ached. The day dragged through the morning hours. Low-hanging clouds threatened snow. The household went about its business as if there were no threat of attack to the men huddled at Whitemarsh in ragged clothes too thin and sparse to keep out the aching cold. Deborah, on fire to know what was happening at the General's camp, was hard put to it, when she had finished her stints of polishing and dusting, to sit quietly at the spinning in the kitchen corner, for she was restless with suspense and curiosity she dared not show since she could not account for it. She found it almost impossible to sit still but she schooled her face and her body to a semblance of repose and managed to let the morning pass. She even remembered to ask about the ailing horse and learned the creature was better thanks to medicine Rob had gone yesterday to a neighboring farm to borrow. So that, she thought, was why he had been upon the woods path. At dinner he didn't look at her at all and she was glad for she thought that meant he in no way connected her with the old woman of yesterday.

When dinner was over she went to the road, hoping Johnny would come with news. But he did not come, and by bedtime her head was, in truth, aching and she was glad to climb again into her great bed.

Again she slept heavily, so heavily that Mistress Teele had to shake her awake the next morning. "Wake up.

Do wake up, Deborah," Ruth Teele said. "William Darragh's come for you and the child. Lydia wants you both with her for Christmas. Hurry now. William's in a fidget, but you'll not be leaving my house without a good breakfast. Susannah's already below-stairs with her father."

Deborah dressed hurriedly, but before she went down she made sure her disguise, hastily bestowed at the bottom of the chest, was hidden in the middle of her belongings. She didn't think anyone would notice she had more to take away than she had brought with her. Anyway, she thought jubilantly, it wouldn't matter now. The message was delivered. Let Rob Bates question her, or wonder! It would do him small good.

But Rob was not in the kitchen when she greeted William Darragh, who explained he wouldn't be taking Will home, for the boy had begged so hard to stay his father hadn't the heart to deny him. Deborah ate an enormous breakfast. Mistress Teele laughed and said a pain in the head must have been good for her appetite. Deborah was bursting to leave, to get back to Philadelphia and discover what had happened. She blessed Lydia for sending for her as she said her good-byes to Mistress Teele and Annie and promised to come back when the Christmas season was over. She felt even better when she saw in the cart William Darragh was driving baskets of food the Teeles were sending their cousins to help out against the shortages in the town.

But when Deborah was again in the city she could not believe what she saw. There seemed to be no change in the place. The same people were going about their businesses in the same way, as if there were no thought of battles possibly being fought so short a distance away. There was nothing in the streets or in the faces of the people upon them to show anything above the ordinary to be happening. William Darragh's slow talk to his daughter gave no sign that he knew of his wife's spying activities and there was something about him that kept Deborah from asking the questions that were bursting her mind. Had she dreamed all that had taken place in the past two days?

It was not until she saw Lydia's face that she knew she had not dreamed it. Waiting for them at the door, Lydia was white, and lines of strain still showing about her eyes and mouth bore witness to the hours when she had not known whether the mission that had, in a sense, been thrust upon her would be successful or, failing, bring trouble upon herself and her whole family. With one arm holding Susannah close against her as if she would never let her go, Lydia reached out the other to Deborah.

"Thee is a true child of liberty, Deborah Stone," she said softly under cover of Susannah's squeals of happiness to be at home again. "We'd best not speak again of what thee did for it's said walls sometimes have ears and what's not said won't be overheard. But the knowledge of thy steadfastness and courage will lie always close to my heart."

Johnny came charging in then from the kitchen and saved Deborah the need to find words of thanks for the praise. But she knew Lydia's words would stay with her forever and would be a rock to lean upon when, in the future, uncertainty of herself threatened her.

Johnny, it appeared, had more curiosity and less caution than his mother. When Deborah was again settled in her old room he asked her to go out with him to walk about the city. When they came to the open space before the State House where they could be sure no one could come within hearing distance without being noticed he said, "*Now* tell me. All of it. Every single thing that happened to thee."

When she had done so she asked him about his mother's activities. He shook his head. "She won't talk about it," he said. "She wasn't stopped. So much I know for she came home with the empty sack she'd taken, full of flour. So she must have gotten to the mill at Frankford. But that's all I *know*. Yet I am sure she got the message to someone who would send it on to General Washington, for once beyond the city nothing would stop her."

"What's happening now?"

"Who can say? There've been rumors a plenty, for I was about the streets when thee came. But one man will say one thing, another the opposite. There's nothing sure nor likely will be today."

And it was, in fact, two more days before they heard the story of what had happened. Then the first units of Howe's army began to drift back to their encampments. It needed no words to tell of their failure, for their sour faces testified that this was a retreating not a victorious army. Then, gradually, the story of the engagement at Whitemarsh got about.

Washington, so far from being surprised, was ready and waiting for the redcoats. McLane's Raiders had tracked Howe's route and the Continental Army, knowing just what to expect down to the last man and gun, and having had many hours to prepare for meeting the enemy, was well entrenched on high ground, their guns placed so as to destroy any effort to approach the camp. Howe's men spent three days trying to find a break in the defending lines, then marched through snow and cold back to the city knowing they had missed a chance to destroy the army and, likely, bring the war to an early end, for if Washington had been defeated that day and his army destroyed, or largely so, it was not likely the remainder of the liberty fighters would have held out long. The British army succeeded in accomplishing only a single thing and that a wanton one. The Hessians, passing the Rising Sun on their return, had deliberately burned it though the Continental soldiers who had been using it had long since left. Deborah was sad at hearing of its destruction. It was, she thought, almost as if the Hessians had destroyed a bit of her own life.

On the night the retreating army came back a British officer appeared at the door of the Darragh home and demanded to see Lydia. Deborah went to the kitchen to fetch her and stood beside her while the redcoat questioned her sternly.

"Mistress Darragh," he said and his voice sent cold shivers up Deborah's back, "on the night we used your front room, did you, as you were bid, send your family to bed before we came?"

"That I did do," Lydia said steadily, firmly meeting his eyes.

"*All* of them?"

"There were only the four of us at the time; my husband, my older son and my daughter, and, of course, myself. The others were visiting relatives in the country. My family remained abovestairs."

"Are you *sure?*"

She stood a little straighter and looked at him with dignity and dislike. "Does thee doubt my word, Captain? Does thee not know I am a Friend? We do not lie."

"No, no," he said, abashed by something in her look. He shook his head, puzzled. "I don't understand it," he went on. "The rebel general knew everything. *Everything,* I tell you. He was ready and waiting and his men grinning like the scarecrows they look from behind their strong barricades. He must have known our forces down to the last gun. Yet no word of our plans was spoken outside this house. *You . . .*" He stared at Lydia as if a new idea had come to him and Deborah thought he's going to ask her if *she* came down. Then what will she say? But the officer dropped his eyes. "*You* were asleep, I know," he said, "for I myself came to get you to lock up after us and I thought I'd never waken you."

"A clean conscience makes a sound sleeper, Captain," Lydia said so meekly Deborah wanted to giggle. "Good day to thee, Captain." Lydia was calmly dismissing him.

"Good day, ma'am," he said and left.

"What will happen now?" Deborah asked Johnny later.

"Who can say, Deborah? The winter's fair set in now. There'll likely be no more fighting till spring. What with the failure to take Washington at Whitemarsh and our victory at Ticonderoga in the north, the British have none so much to be thankful for. Ebenezer Jordan says the General has sent some of his men to build huts against the cold at the Valley Forge. Likely he'll go into winter quarters there when all is ready. It'll be a lean winter for the army, I'm thinking. Come spring—well, there do be some say our Ben Franklin has persuaded the French to send us help. Please Heaven old Howe'll have got wind of it and think he's had enough and will take himself off. We can but wait and see."

"Pray God you be right, Johnny," Deborah said, and felt in her bones he would be. Some day—months, maybe years from now—the war would be over and Uncle Matt would come home. She would tell him of her small part in it and he would be proud of her. She wondered what he would do about Sophronisba and, for a breath, felt the old fears of the Woman come upon her. Then she lifted her shoulders and grinned to herself, knowing that Sophronisba Albright would never again be able to terrify her; guessing that once anyone could stand, unafraid before her, the Old Cow's power to hurt would disappear as a mist before a strong wind. She's nothing but an old bully, Deborah thought. Why was I ever so frightened of her?

She started to sing, softly, to herself, increasing the tempo and volume of the song until it became a

triumphant affirmation of her faith in the eventual
success of their fight for freedom and equality between
men:

> Through the woods we go
> And through the boggy mire
> Straightway till we come to our hearts' desire.
> Oh dooley, dooley dey
> Oh, the little dooley dey.

HISTORICAL NOTE

Much of JOURNEY INTO DANGER is history and many
of the people described in it were real people. The
Darragh family did live in Philadelphia, in the Loxley
House near Bathsheba's Bath and Bower, in the hard
winter of 1777–1778. There are records to show that
Lydia Darragh, though a Quaker, did indeed spy for
General Washington, sending messages sewed inside
buttons to her elder son, Charles, by her younger son,
Johnny. She did overhear the complete details of
General Howe's plans to capture Washington and his
army, by surprise, at Whitemarsh. And she did carry
word of those details to one of Washington's officers
near Frankford's Mill.

These things she told to her daughter, Ann, and that
tale was later written down and may be found today
in *The Philadelphia Historical Magazine*, Vol. I, pp.
377–403.

Deborah is not a "real" character. But, while Lydia

was telling one officer of her discoveries of Howe's plans, another officer, General Budinot, was reading a copy of them at the Rising Sun Tavern. This copy, as Budinot tells it in his *Journal*, was given him by "a little, poor-looking, insignificant, old woman" who could not have been Lydia. Nobody has ever discovered who that little old woman was. She came to be, in my mind, Deborah Stone, masquerading as an old crone.

Rob Bates, too, is an imaginary character. But he is based on stories told by other young men who were as opposed as he was, though without his wildness, to the Continental Cause.

About the author

Nancy Faulkner is both a meticulous historian and a superb storyteller, who knows how to maintain suspense to the last page. The author of many popular books, including *Knights Besieged, The Yellow Hat,* and *The Traitor Queen,* she brings the period and her characters vividly to life, whether she's writing about ancient Crete, first-century England, sixteenth-century Rhodes, or eighteenth-century America. A graduate of Wellesley College, she received her M.A. degree in history at Cornell and later taught history at Sweet Briar College. Miss Faulkner now lives in New York City, where she pursues a full-time writing career.

H19

THE
RISING SUN TAVERN

DATE DUE

DEBORAH ON

TEELE FARM

SCHUYLKILL RIVER

GAYLORD   PRINTED IN U.S.A.

REFUGEES ESCAPING THE
BRITISH

DELAWARE RIVER